MURDER
AT
FERRY CREEK

Book Six In The
O'Toole/Starker
Murder Mystery Series

G. A. Cockerham

Published by Lands End Publishing

ISBN-13: 978-1-7339973-6-2

Acclaim for G. A. Cockerham's mysteries

—Featured in Who's Who/What's What Book Picks
in *Southern Oregon* Magazine.

Amazon Reviews:

Murder On The Oregon Coast

Interesting story lines. Good flow into the next story. Kept me guessing who was guilty.

Will definitely seek out other books by this writer.

Police procedural in a small town detective story with brilliant deductive work.

Murder On The Wind

This is another great book by the author. The cover and title make it irresistible, and the story is very intriguing. Not sure where it was going next. It's "murder light", with no sex or explicit violence, just great characters and story. LOVE the local references to our little corner of paradise on the south coast. Two thumbs way up!

Murder Replete…*for now*

I just finished reading 1-3 of this series, and all I have to say is wow! This series was so thrilling, and kept me wanting to read more. You can tell that everything put into this book was researched and thought out thoroughly to make it seem like it was more "real life". I can't wait until more books from the author come out, I'll be one of the first to snag them.

Murder Takes All

I have read all the O'Toole/Starker Murder Mystery Series. This was a "could not put down" book.

Great book! … written with interesting twists, turns and surprises

Murder At Macklyn Cove

A friend gifted me Georgia Cockerham's set of murder mysteries since we live right in Brookings where they take place! It was such a kick to read about the detectives stopping at local restaurants for lunch and going on hikes where we hike! Georgia gives some of the history of various places too, all the while twisting the plot and always surprising me in the end. A great read!

Also by G. A. Cockerham

O'TOOLE/STARKER
OREGON COAST MURDER MYSTERIES

Murder On The Oregon Coast

Murder On The Wind

Murder Replete…*for now*

Murder Takes All

Murder at Macklyn Cove

Acknowledgements

No one writes a good book without input from others. Listed below are the names of several people whose expertise contributed greatly to the authenticity and human-interest aspects of my mystery by providing input based upon personal experience. To each I give my gratitude.

I would not be writing murder mysteries without the assistance of my husband, Bruce Cockerham. He edits my law enforcement references, provides ideas, and is my constant source of support and encouragement. Bruce is a retired police captain with thirty years of experience in law enforcement. He's worked in patrol, traffic, detectives, SWAT, administration, and as an academy instructor. Bruce trained with the FBI as a counter sniper and is a graduate of both the California Command College and the FBI National Academy. He holds a BA from Whitworth University and an MDiv from the San Francisco Theological Seminary.

Forensic DNA expert Camilla Green provides me with little-known forensic techniques. Cami's expertise has placed her in several television shows including *Cold Justice, Cold Justice: Sex Crimes, On the Case with Paula Zahn,* and *Murder Decoded.*

Brad Alcorn retired from the Fresno, CA Police Department after thirty-four years of service. Fifteen of those years he served on the prestigious SWAT Team. His assignments included working as a canine handler, sniper, team leader, undercover, Violent Crime Suppression Unit, HEAT (Help Eliminate Auto Theft), and Career Criminal Auto Theft Team (CCATT). Brad worked eight years as a detective and night detective with assignments in robbery, patrol, sexual assault, and homicide.

Brad is currently a County Commissioner for Curry County, OR and is a past City Counselor for Brookings, OR.

A part of Brad's personal life few in Brookings may know is that he was the trainer and manager for the undefeated, three-time lightweight world boxing champion Jenifer Alcorn, his wife.

Dani Melin is a freelance, multi-talented illustrator and graphic designer living and working in Minnesota. Dani's cover art has been showcased on my last four Oregon Coast murder mystery books. In addition to creating cover art and book illustrations, she excels in illustrative logo branding, and creative marketing. She also loves creating editorial and beauty illustrations. To view and learn more about Dani's work, visit her website at www.danimelindesign.com.

TABLE OF CONTENTS

Acknowledgements   vii

CHAPTER 1   1

CHAPTER 2   5

CHAPTER 3   9

CHAPTER 4   15

CHAPTER 5   25

CHAPTER 6   33

CHAPTER 7   43

CHAPTER 8   45

CHAPTER 9   57

CHAPTER 10   63

CHAPTER 11   65

CHAPTER 12   71

CHAPTER 13   83

CHAPTER 14   87

CHAPTER 15   95

CHAPTER 16   105

CHAPTER 17   111

CHAPTER 18   119

CHAPTER 19   127

CHAPTER 20   129

CHAPTER 21   135

CHAPTER 22   143

CHAPTER 23   149

CHAPTER 24   155

CHAPTER 25   163

CHAPTER 26   171

CHAPTER 27   181

CHAPTER 28   187

CHAPTER 29   197

CHAPTER 30   201

CHAPTER 31   203

CHAPTER 1

The sleek F-Type Jaguar pulled into the lot and parked. A reserved parking sign read "CLW." The space was one of three reserved for the broker-owner and two agents at a downtown real estate firm. The car door slowly opened, and two long legs swung out, supported by four-inch candy-apple high heels. She was dressed in a tailored black business suit, and her purse was a perfect match for the shoes. Three spaces away, a middle-aged man getting out of his car stopped to take in the young beauty.

Crystal had come a long way in ten years, working her way up from a fledgling real estate agent living on Top Ramen and rice to owner of one of the most successful real estate firms in the state of Oregon.

The upscale company's office was nestled in among several commercial businesses. It was prime real estate in the center of town. The glass front windows displayed photos of southern Oregon coast homes for sale, each with its own description. Inside, the lobby walls displayed evidence of Crystal's superior skills. She'd won numerous sales awards, most within the past five years.

The statuesque woman entered through beveled glass doors. She glanced into the offices of her two top agents, each talking with prospective buyers, and paused to observe the bullpen where eight desks were tightly arranged. Three were occupied by agents on their phones. A whiteboard on the wall reported that the other five were out showing property.

Crystal sat down in her plush European leather chair and listened to the messages on her desk phone. The first was from her husband.

"Crystal, this is Grant. We'll never finish this if you keep avoiding me. We're just adding to the wealth of our attorneys. Let's sit down and discuss how we can divide our assets and be done with it all."

Before returning Grant's call, Crystal left a voice mail for her attorney. "What is holding you up, Wade? It's been two years since the papers were signed. I'm tired of waiting. You need to finalize this divorce now. Give him more money if that's what it takes. There's only one thing he can't have, and you know what it is. Just get it done."

Crystal inhaled deeply and thought about what she would say to the man for whom she no longer had any use. She called and was greeted with a familiar recorded message. *This is Grant Wellingham. Sorry I missed your call. I'm tied up now. Leave your name and number and I'll get back to you.*

Crystal heard the beep and responded, "Grant, sorry I missed your call. Come to my office at eleven and we can talk. I haven't changed my mind about the business, but I know that we both must compromise. So I can probably be more generous with our other assets. I need to know what it will take to end this. We both want out of our misery."

At eleven, Grant sat down across from Crystal in her office. "You're looking good, Crystal. Business must be great."

"It's a product of hard work, Grant. My hard work."

Grant sat back in his chair and smiled. "I've worked hard too, Crystal. It's because of me that you were able to start this business. Remember? It took me building four houses to make the money needed to lease this building, furnish it, and keep you above water as you acquired enough agents to cover your bills. You wouldn't be here today if it weren't for me." Grant leaned forward. "And legally, this business is half mine."

Crystal placed both hands palms-down on top of her desk. "Okay, Grant, let's discuss this like two adults." She took time to compose herself. "It's not my intent to take it all." She laughed. "It won't be like that song about the wife getting the gold mine and the husband the shaft. Do you remember that song, Grant? We used to laugh when we'd hear it at that little country bar we liked.

No, I don't want us to be anything like that. I'll call my attorney and let him know that I'm giving you the house and the truck. We have a few hundred thousand in savings. You can take half of that too, Grant. I'm willing to give it to you so that we can keep this friendly and civil. Why don't I call now and ask Wade to draw up the agreement? We can finally settle and go our separate ways."

Grant sat silently through Crystal's rambling response. A sneer slowly spread across his face. "That's very generous of you, Crystal. To tell you the truth, I'm surprised. You almost sound like you care. I like that you want this to end friendly. You and me remaining friends will make it much easier for our business partnership. I'm not interested in the house. It would only hold memories of you. And I'd take the truck under any circumstances. You know what I want."

Crystal remained silent as Grant's sneer became a relaxed smile. He laughed with arrogance. "We're going to be business partners. Split right down the middle."

Crystal's entire body tensed. She stood up and spoke through gritted teeth. "We'll never be business partners. I built this business, and I intend to keep it. All of it! One hundred percent! You can have the house, the truck, and half of our savings. Heck, instead of joint custody, I'll even give you the kids. But my business is not open for negotiation. You need to take my offer and sign the paperwork, Grant, or I promise you'll be sorry."

Grant chuckled. "So now you're threatening me?" He stood up to leave and leaned forward with his hands on her desk. "I'm in no hurry, Crystal. I'm willing to wait until you come around."

CHAPTER 2

The abandoned house was off a dirt road a few miles from the highway and looked like something out of a ghost town movie set. What little grass grew was overgrown with weeds and berry bushes. A rain gutter hung from the roof. Plywood covered up two of the side windows, and a sheet had been hung inside to block the view of anyone coming to the front door. Chipped paint and a broken porch railing completed the picture of neglect.

Blake drove his old Ford Ranger down the dusty road and parked. He walked up three steps, put his key in the lock, and entered. With a flip of the switch, he turned on a single bulb in a corner lamp that had long ago lost its shade. He walked into the kitchen where another naked bulb hung, perused the refrigerator's contents, and removed a can of beer and an open bag of chips. He carried them into the sparsely-furnished living room.

An old recliner was positioned for watching the TV that sat across the room on an open TV tray. A coffee table was situated in front of the recliner and a second, smaller table stood against a wall. Blake lowered himself into the recliner. He took a long swig of beer before setting the can down on the table in front of him. A stack of small papers and a bag of grass were also on the table. He carefully rolled a joint and lit it. Then he picked up the TV remote and pushed the power button. An early episode of *Forensic Files* came up on the screen. He silenced his cell phone and proceeded to drink and inhale his lunch. A short time later his phone lit up. Blake recognized the number. "Yeah?"

"It's me, man. I'm in a bad way. You got anything for me?"

"You got money?"

"Yeah, I can pay."

"Bring it over in thirty minutes."

Blake ended the call, took a swig of beer, and dragged hard on his joint when the phone lit up again. He looked at caller ID and answered.

"Mrs. Anderson, how are you today?"

"I'm well, thank you, Blake. I'm calling to ask if you'd have time to work in my yard today. Company is coming this weekend, and I'd like for the yard to look nice."

"Sure I can, Mrs. Anderson. I'll be over this afternoon."

"Thank you, Blake. I always know that I can count on you."

"Yes, you can, Mrs. Anderson."

Blake took another drag on the joint. He smiled with pride at how successful he'd become at manipulating people. His thoughts were interrupted by a knock on the front door. He walked over to the door and looked through the peephole he'd put in. On the top step stood a young man with his head down and hands in his pockets. "Yeah?"

"I've got the money."

"Show me."

Shifting his weight back and forth, the customer pulled his right hand out with a folded wad of bills.

Blake opened the door and allowed room for the man to step in long enough to complete the deal and leave. He had just sat down when his phone lit up a third time. He knew who was calling. "Yeah?"

"Blake, it's me. I need your help with something. I don't want to talk about it over the phone. Meet me at our regular spot in an hour."

"What is it you want, Crystal? I'm just getting comfortable here."

"I don't want to talk about it over the phone. Just meet me."

Blake was silent.

Crystal spoke again. "Will you be there?"

"Yeah. One hour."

At the designated time, Blake parked on the side of the road and walked into the forest about twenty feet to where Crystal was waiting.

"Hi, Blake. It's been a while. How are you?"

"What do you want, Crystal?"

"It's Grant," said Crystal. "He's gone off the rails. I don't know if it's heroin or meth, but I can't take it anymore. We're in the middle of a divorce, and he won't settle. I offered a friendly settlement, but he wants half my business. I don't want him as a partner, and there's no way I'm going to sell."

Blake listened as he lit a cigarette. "You dragged me out here to tell me you're getting a divorce? I know you're lying about Grant being into drugs, but I wouldn't care if he was. I don't care what shape Grant, or your marriage, is in."

"I want him to disappear, Blake."

Blake took another drag and slowly blew out the smoke. "Well, Crystal. No can do. You see, I've settled down and I'm making a decent living. I live in a nice apartment with a church-going girlfriend who knows me as a successful handyman. I found an abandoned house a while back, and it's perfect for my business dealings. My girlfriend figures I travel a lot with my work. She's introduced me to a bunch of church-going customers who think I'm an honest, God-fearing man. My drug business generously supplements my income, and I'm staying under the radar of the cops. I don't want to mess things up."

Crystal laughed. "You mean you've become a better manipulator of people."

"Call it what you want, Crystal. They all swallow what I tell them, hook, line, and sinker."

Crystal looked down, then back up at Blake. "Are you telling me no, Blake? Because if that's what you are doing, I think you're forgetting our past relationship that went beyond a simple business transaction. Maybe I need to jar your memory. It wasn't that long ago. I've still got the evidence, Blake. Evidence that could put you away for a very long time."

Blake stared at Crystal and said nothing.

"Look," she said. "I don't want to waste your time, so let me be blunt. I own you, Blake."

Blake threw his cigarette butt down and ground it into the dirt. "Do you have a plan?"

Crystal smiled. "That's better. Yes, I do. I'll tell you about it tomorrow. Come to my office in the morning."

"I'll need help."

"I know, and I've got just the guy."

Blake turned around and walked back to his car.

CHAPTER 3

Kevin sat back in his chair, a blue Adirondack, on his second-floor deck. The same style chair in yellow was artfully placed beside it. He looked out at the grounds of his condo association, an expansive lawn kept green year-round and a few cottonwoods with leaves that shimmered in the breeze. A small stream burbled as it meandered between the buildings. Kevin admired the beauty and sound of his surroundings and contemplated how fortunate he was. The condo, his BMW, and his trophy wife were all the results of his job. He believed that he was good at what he did, but he knew that it was his loyal relationship with his boss that kept him in six figures.

His thoughts were interrupted by a call on the cell phone sitting on the arm of his chair. He picked up the phone and looked at caller ID.

"Hi, Crystal."

"Hi, Kevin. Do you have a minute?"

"Sure. I'm just sitting on my deck hoping that Bella comes home on time today. What's up?"

Crystal's voice sounded strained. "I have a business request. Something I'd like you to help me with. I'll pay you handsomely for the help. It's not something I want to discuss over the phone. I'm in your neighborhood, just finishing up some shopping. Would it be convenient for me to stop by now?"

Kevin stood up and walked to the balcony railing. "Help you, Crystal? Of course I'll help, and you don't have to pay me. You've done a lot for me and my career. I'm expecting Bella home in about forty-five minutes. At least, I'm hoping she'll be home. She's been coming home later and later. Do you need more than forty-five minutes?"

"Forty-five minutes should be more than enough for what I want to discuss. I'll see you in a few."

Kevin went downstairs. The sound of tires on the gravel driveway let him know that Crystal had arrived. He opened the front door. "That was fast."

Crystal smiled as she sauntered past Kevin into the condo. "I told you that I was in the neighborhood."

Kevin closed the door and followed his boss into the living room. "If you'd rather, we could sit on the upstairs deck."

"No, the couch is fine."

Kevin picked up his beer. "I had just popped the top when you called. Can I get you something to drink? Beer, wine, ice water?"

Crystal smiled. "Thank you, Kevin, but I'm fine. Please sit down and enjoy your beer."

Kevin sat in a chair opposite the couch. "So, what is it I can help you with?"

Crystal explained her dilemma and the help she needed. "I'll pay you twenty thousand dollars to help me out, Kevin. That should pay off your car."

Kevin stood up and walked across the room. "I don't know what to say, Crystal. I would like to help you like I did before, but I wasn't married then. I can't do what you're asking. I have Bella to think about now."

Crystal picked up her purse in preparation for leaving. "I imagine Bella might enjoy a vacation with you someplace in the Caribbean, or maybe a shopping spree? I'll make it twenty-five thousand."

Kevin looked down at the floor. "Twenty-five thousand. That's a lot of money. But what you're asking… I just don't know."

Crystal interrupted him. "Let's both sleep on this, and we'll talk again tomorrow. I can't think clearly when I'm tired, and I don't expect you can either."

Kevin shook his head. "Okay. But sleeping on it isn't going to change my mind."

"We'll discuss this again tomorrow, Kevin. Try and get some rest. Oh, and Kevin."

"Yeah?"

"This stays between us. Don't tell anyone, including Bella. Do you understand?"

"Yeah."

Crystal left, and Kevin sent Bella a text message. *There's something I really need to discuss with you. Please stop whatever you're working on and come home. Or at least text me and let me know when I can expect you. This is important, Bella.*

* * *

Kevin arrived at his office the next morning looking disheveled and unkept. He poured himself a cup of coffee, sat down at his desk, and stared at the text message from Bella. He read it again, trying to think about what it meant and what he should do next.

Hi Kevin. I got in late last night. You were sleeping so hard that I didn't have the heart to wake you, so I slept on the couch. I left for the office early this morning. Just letting you know I'll be working late again this evening.

He thought about his wife's new work schedule and decided to call rather than return the text. Four rings and his call went to her voice mail.

"Bella, we need to talk. You working late every night isn't good for our marriage. It's not good for me. It's not just your work we need to talk about. Something's come up related to work that I want to discuss with you. Let me know that you've received this and that you can make it home on time."

Kevin glanced at the files on his desk and thought again about returning Crystal's text. He was considering what to do next when he heard the receptionist greet someone walking in. He stepped out of his office.

"Hello, I'm Kevin Lacky. What can we do for you today?"

* * *

The day remained busy though Kevin had a hard time concentrating on work. He finished with his last client and arrived home about six. He opened a can of beer and sent a text to his wife.

Since I haven't heard from you, I'm guessing that you're working late again. I just got home. Got time for a quick chat?

Thirty minutes went by with no response. Kevin sent another text. *At least let me know that you got my text.*

Twenty minutes later, he got into his car and drove to his wife's place of employment. He found the building locked up tight and no lights on. He returned home and opened another beer.

At ten after eight Kevin's trophy wife walked through the front door. She walked up to him and kissed him on the cheek. "Hello, dear. Sorry I had to work late again. The boss had me typing a letter for him. It was long enough to be a novel. He wanted it done before I went home. I would love a glass of wine. Did you eat?"

Kevin sat down on the couch. "You can get your own wine, dear," he said, emphasizing the last word. "What's going on, Bella?"

Bella stepped into the kitchen, poured herself a glass of Chardonnay, and walked back into the living room. "I just had to work late. That's all."

Kevin stood up. "This is not the first time you've come home late. In fact, in the past three months you've been late far more often than you've arrived home on time. I sent you a text message about six and again at half-past. When you didn't respond, I drove to your office. It was locked up tight and totally dark inside. You weren't there, Bella. Now, will you answer me? What's going on?"

Bella sipped her wine. "I don't want to talk about this right now. I'm tired and going to bed."

Kevin turned red and balled his fists. "I've given you a car, half-ownership in this condo, and a luxury vacation for each of the past two years. What is it that's missing in your life? If you're having an affair, Bella, I want a divorce."

Bella stopped in the kitchen to top off her wine. She turned to Kevin and smiled. "You won't divorce me, Kevin. Not unless you're ready to start all over. You said it yourself. I own half of this condo and my car. I also have a right to spousal support since you make far more than I do. Now that I think about it, I might be better off without you. But don't worry. I'm very comfortable the way things are, and I don't want to move." She turned and started to walk away.

Kevin clenched his teeth and then yelled out, "We'll see about that."

Bella abruptly turned around and faced him. "Oh, and, Kevin, don't ever text me again when I've told you I'm working late."

Kevin finished his beer and poured himself a glass of bourbon. He grabbed his phone and punched in the number of his broker. Crystal answered.

"Good evening, Kevin. Ready to talk about what we discussed?"

"Yes, I am. And I need to talk with you about my own situation. I just learned that Bella's having an affair. I need to talk with you tonight."

"It's a little late to talk now, Kevin. Let's get together at the office in the morning."

"Look, Crystal, I really need to talk tonight. I can't relax. I feel like my life is beginning to unravel and it's Bella's fault. She doesn't love me anymore. Maybe she never did. This won't wait until morning. And remember that little errand you wanted me to do for you? Well, I've changed my mind, and you don't need to pay me. But I need to talk with you tonight. I'll be there in twenty minutes."

Kevin drove to Crystal's home. She answered the door in pale pink sweatpants and a hoodie. He walked past her and into the living room. She closed the door and followed.

"I'm glad you've changed your mind."

"Well, I need your help with something too. I can't remain married to Bella, and I can't file for divorce without her taking most of what I have. You know, before we married, she was a shy, sweet person who told me she wanted to spend the rest of her life with me. She talked about wanting children and a little house with a fenced backyard for the kids. Once we married, she changed. Kids were no longer on her radar. That came as a shock to me since I wanted a family, but I told her we'd wait. We don't have a house yet, but our condo is great, and I wanted to build up our savings before buying anything more expensive. I bought her a car, but she has never been satisfied. Then she started working late, and last night she threatened me. Look, Crystal." Kevin paused and walked across the room before continuing. "Bella has turned into a manipulative, cruel user of people, especially me. I can't live like this anymore."

Crystal got up and walked to the bar. She held up a tumbler and a bottle of Jameson whiskey. "I sense that you could use a drink."

Kevin was pacing the floor. "Sure."

Crystal poured a couple of drinks and carried them across the room. She handed one to Kevin and sat down on the couch. "What is it, exactly, that you want me to do?"

Kevin swirled the ice cube in his glass. "A little quid pro quo. I want you to get rid of her for me."

Crystal set her glass down on the coffee table. "Get rid of her?"

Kevin stared at Crystal before responding. "Just like the problem you've asked my help with. You want Grant out of your life, and I want Bella out of mine."

Crystal sipped again on her drink. "That's a pretty extreme solution to your problem, Kevin. With Grant and me it's different. We're talking about millions of dollars and my business. You can just divorce Bella and start over again. Trust me, that will be far easier on you than spending the rest of your life in prison. You don't want to be found guilty of murder."

Kevin shook his head. "No, that's just it. I will never be found guilty because I'm not the one who's going to kill her. That will be the friend you've hired to take care of Grant. He can do for me what he's going to do for you."

Crystal stood up and walked to the bar. She set down her empty glass.

"No. I can tell you for certain we won't have two deaths from the same cause. That would be a mistake. I've got an idea. But you must be patient. Everything has to be carefully planned. I'll have Blake call soon with what we need from you."

"How do I know you'll help me after I help you with Grant?"

"You'll have to trust me, Kevin."

CHAPTER 4

The signs of spring were everywhere along the southern Oregon coast. Purple crocuses, yellow daffodils, and blue bearded iris created splashes of color in many front yards. It's a welcome sight after a long, wet, gray winter.

Along the exposed rocky shoreline, a low tide unfolds a beautiful array of orange, red, and purple sea stars and fluorescent green sea anemones. Spring is a time for long walks on the beach, striking sunsets, and daytime activity at the Port of Brookings Harbor.

The southern Oregon coast is known for its offshore giant rock formations known as sea stacks. Scattered up the coastline, these historical rocks are reminders of an ancient time when the mainland extended further into the ocean. These remnants of the rocky headlands were eroded over millions of years through wave action and earth movement.

Downtown, a block off the main highway, which is also known as Chetco Avenue, stands a single-story, U-shaped building housing offices for city hall, fire, and police. In a corner office at the police station, Detective Patty O'Toole sat at her desk enjoying her first cup of coffee for the day as she listened to several voice mail messages. Caffeine with two creams and some sugar are her morning pick-me-up. Her partner, Detective Rick Starker, sat opposite Patty. He too was drinking coffee, black. Next to his mug was a very important white bakery bag. It held his breakfast. Within the department, Rick is known for his appetite for pastries. Across the state, the two detectives are known for their success rate with solving homicides.

Patty set her cup on the desk. "Thought I'd take a collection today and buy a birthday cake for Brad. Any idea what flavor he'd like?"

Rick put down his bacon-topped bar and swallowed. "No. I'm sure anything will be okay."

Patty's cell phone rang, putting an end to the cake-flavor discussion. "Where? Okay. Rick and I will drive out there now." She ended the call and stood up. "The Public Works Director, George, called in. Says there's a barrel that has emerged up at Ferry Creek Dam. Figures its surfacing is due to a decline in the water level. He and the guy who first saw it removed the lid. It appears to hold human bones and some kind of liquid."

Rick ate the last bit of his pastry. He put on his jacket and confirmed with his elbow that his gun was in the holster, a habit due to an incident some years prior. "I'll drive."

Patty smiled. "Works for me."

Rick drove through the town of Brookings, a typical older community with a four-lane road and no continuity to the aesthetics of the commercial area. Each business has its own look, façade, and paint color, and there are few retailers compared to the number of offices. He turned on Old County Road and again on Marine Drive. The private road to the dam was gated, but George had left it open in anticipation of the detectives' arrival.

Rick proceeded up the road to the dam. "It's beautiful out here, but this road is sure rough. Does the city maintain it?"

"My understanding is that they are out here a couple times a year to keep the road clear."

Rick looked toward Patty. "So, Detective O'Toole, you're the history buff. Can you tell me anything about the Ferry Creek Dam?"

She smiled. "You're in luck, Detective Starker. I've lived my entire life here on the coast and I learned about the Ferry Creek Dam while in school. I'll talk while you watch the road. A car went over the side and into the ravine not too long ago."

As the reservoir came into view, Patty continued. "This was once Brookings' water supply. Over the years the city has discussed whether to remove the dam or restore it. If restored, it would provide a redundant water source."

Rick pointed to a structure in the water. "What's that used for?"

"That serves as a temporary home to some of the hatchery baby salmon called smolt. It becomes a floating pen when nets are connected to all four sides. An additional net can be strung across the top to keep out predators. Each year tens of thousands of smolt are brought here to Brookings. Most are placed directly into the Chetco River. A smaller quantity is placed into that pen to acclimate before their final release into the river. The ODFW and the South Coast Fishermen created the net pen about twelve years ago as part of a research experiment. I've read where the need to differentiate between the fish placed directly into the river and those brought up here to the pen first is managed by a wire tag system. Clipping the adipose fin is a second required action. That procedure distinguishes the wild salmon from those started out in a hatchery or acclimation pen."

"That's new to me," said Rick. "I've never really understood what went on here with the fish. It's interesting."

"I think so," said Patty. "But let's change the subject for a while and talk with George about this barrel."

Rick nodded. "Yeah. It looks like we have a probable homicide to investigate." He pulled off behind a parked Brookings city vehicle.

The detectives stepped out of the car as George walked up to Patty and pointed toward the barrel.

"It's about half full of some sort of liquid. If it was full when it was rolled into the lake, a lot has leaked out. Looks like human bones inside."

Rick walked over and looked inside the large container. He called to Patty, "Are we missing anyone?"

Patty shook her head. "No one's been recently reported missing." She walked over to join Rick at the barrel, then turned back to the city employee. "Did you touch anything?"

"No." He nodded to the guy standing next to the director's car. "His name's Boyd. He's a volunteer with the Oregon South Coast Fishermen organization and came out here to check on road access and the pen. He found the barrel and called me. We got it out of the water, set it upright, and then pried the lid off."

Patty glanced at Rick and then back to George. "It's good that you didn't stick your hand in and test the water. I'm guessing this is some kind of acid solution. You need to get a HAZMAT team up here. Ask them to call me when they're done."

George nodded and took out his cell phone.

"There's nothing more we can do," Rick said to Patty. "Not until the coroner examines the bones and the fluid is tested." He looked at Boyd, the volunteer. "Was the lid difficult to remove?"

The man shrugged. "Not at all. I don't think it was fully secured before being rolled into the water."

"Thanks," said Patty.

She and Rick returned to the car and started back to the office. She continued giving Rick information about the dam and reservoir.

"In 2012 we had a storm that dropped several inches of rain in a very short period of time. It rained so hard that the water flowed over the dam, across this road, and into Ferry Creek."

"That's a lot of water. I've not experienced rain like that since moving here from Boston, and that was a decade ago. The dam seems to serve a purpose, so why dismantle it? How much discussion has there been on what action to take?"

"According to my research, the city has explored what to do. One study estimated the removal cost to be $2.9 million. The price tag increased to $8.8 million to relocate the spillway, and realign and expand the dam. The state now considers it hazardous to downstream property owners. An inspection revealed a gully on the downstream side, indicating an overtopping event which could result in damage or catastrophic failure of the dam. Uphill slope movement is also affecting the dam's integrity."

"So, after all of that, did they make a decision?"

"They did. In 2018, city staff recommended no action until federal dollars could be made available. I've learned recently that federal funding for dismantling the dam has come through."

Rick pulled into the parking lot. "Who funds the fish project?"

"ODFW provides funding, and volunteers do all the work."

Rick turned the car off. "Oregon Department of Fish and Wildlife. Thanks for the history lesson."

"Anytime. So, I've been meaning to ask you, what do you think of the new chief?"

Rick shrugged his shoulders. "Not much yet to think about. He's only been here a couple of weeks. Came from some department up north." He paused and then asked, "What do you think of him?"

"He seems to be interested in the job." A smile spread across Patty's face. "He complimented me and you on all the cases we've solved together and asked what our secret is."

Rick laughed softly. "Our secret?"

"Yeah, as though we had some special powers or method relating to the cases we've solved."

"Did you tell him it's just good old-fashioned detective work?"

"I did, but he didn't look convinced."

"Hmmmm. That reminds me of something I did in Boston."

Patty was intrigued. "Something you did? What was it?"

Rick grinned. "Let me think about it for a while. Whether it will work. I'll tell you this afternoon."

"Okay. You've piqued my curiosity."

Patty and Rick had just sat down at their desks when Officer Burt Bradley, known in the department as Brad, came to the office door.

Patty looked up. "Hey, Brad."

"Hey, Patty."

When Brad did not continue, Patty asked, "What's up?"

"I just cited a guy who complained the whole time I was with him."

Patty smiled at Brad. "That happens a lot in your job."

"Yeah, but this felt different."

Patty lifted her eyebrows. "Different? How?"

Brad looked around the office while thinking about how to proceed. He looked at Patty. "He was half right."

Patty waited for Brad to continue.

"I know it sounds funny, but I understood why he was complaining."

Patty put down her pencil and turned her chair toward Brad, who had sat down on a seat against the wall. "Tell me about it."

"Okay. So this Nissan passes me going north on Chetco from Harbor. He was going 40 miles an hour in the 20-mile-per-hour zone. I lit up the car and stopped him." Brad took a breath and continued. "The guy pulled over and rolled down his window. I let him know why I'd stopped him and then asked for his license, registration, and insurance. He starts talking as he's getting the registration and insurance certificates out of the glove box. He says, 'Oh, I thought maybe I have a taillight out.'

"I took his registration and license back to my car and called it in. The guy had no priors. I returned the license and registration to him and told him again that he was going 40 in a 20-mile-per-hour zone. That's when he started complaining."

Patty smiled. "Why was this stop different from the hundreds you've made before?"

Brad raised his hands, palms toward Patty. "Let me finish. So the guy says, 'Twenty-mile-per-hour zone? I came across the bridge and the sign said 35 miles per hour.'

"I told him that there was another sign about a block further up the street that reads 20 miles per hour.

"'My God,' he said. 'You are telling me that within one city block, there are two different speed-limit signs? I know that if I keep driving north on Chetco, the speed limit changes to 30 miles per hour and then, within a short distance while still on Chetco Avenue, it changes to 35 miles per hour. What is the purpose of changing the speed limit four times within two or three miles?'"

Patty continued to listen to Brad. "What did you tell him?"

Brad looked down at his hands and then up to Patty. "I told him that he was going 40, which is over the speed limit no matter where on Chetco he was, and 20 miles over the speed limit at the location I stopped him. I filled out the ticket and handed it to him. Told him he could either pay or make a court date."

"Okay," Patty said. "So you stopped a motorist going 20 miles over the speed limit. Why was this so hard?"

Brad slapped his hands on his thighs. "Because, Patty, I too wonder why we've got four different speed limits just to drive through town. Did anyone think about how this affects the locals, not to mention the tourists? I felt kind of bad about ticketing the guy because he was half right."

Patty sat back in her chair. "Not our problem, Brad. We don't make the laws. We just enforce them. That driver will move through town a little more carefully next time."

Brad looked over at Rick, who had his head down, writing a report, then back to Patty. "Yeah, you're right. Thanks for listening."

After Brad left, Patty glanced at Rick, knowing he'd heard all of Brad's story. Although he didn't lift his head, Patty could see the corners of Rick's mouth turned up into a smile. She picked up her pencil and continued writing a report. Then her cell phone rang. She looked at caller ID and answered.

"Detective O'Toole."

"Detective O'Toole, this is your mother, and I just love it when I hear you answer the phone that way. Do you have a minute?"

Patty laughed. "I know you do, Mom. I do have a minute. How's the day going for you?"

"I'm taking line dancing, and we danced to a song I'd not heard before. It was hard to pay attention to the dance steps because I was trying to listen to the words to the song."

"Line dancing! That's great. What's the name of the song?"

"I can't think of it right now, but it's something about staying out of AA. I'll write down the name and the singer for the next time we talk. The music is great, and the lyrics are very creative."

"Staying out of AA, and it's a funny song. I look forward to hearing about it. Everything else okay?"

"Well, let me think. I exercised this morning at the senior center. Then went to lunch with my friend Jessica. She's a writer and I love to read, so we always have something to talk about.

"There's another part of the conversation that Jessica and I had that I'd like to share with you. It's hilarious. I don't want to be too much of an interruption while you're working, so I'll tell you another time."

"I'd like to hear about it, Mom. Let's go to lunch one day next week."

"That would be great. You and Rick stay safe."

"Love you too, Mom."

After the call, Patty got up from her desk. "Things are pretty quiet right now, so I'll let the LT know about the barrel with the bones."

Rick nodded. "I'm going to eventually finish this report. When you're done talking with the LT, want to hear what I have in mind for the new chief?"

"Oh, yeah."

Patty walked down the hall to the lieutenant's office. The blinds across its two large glass windows were open, allowing the lieutenant to see Patty before she entered. "Hello, O'Toole." The lieutenant had never addressed Patty by her first name. He was a serious man who spent all of his time with family when not working. The wall behind him was evidence of his involvement with Special Olympics, 4-H, and FFA.

Patty stepped inside the office. "Hi, LT. Got a minute?"

The lieutenant closed the file he'd been reading and sat back in his chair. "I do."

Patty sat down. "Rick and I were out at the old Ferry Creek Dam a while ago. Someone had noticed a barrel floating in the water and called Public Works. George, with the city, helped the guy remove the lid from the barrel and then called us. Inside the barrel were what appear to be human bones in some kind of solution."

"HAZMAT called?"

"Yes. And the bones and solution are on their way to the medical examiner and lab."

The lieutenant nodded. "Any idea who the bones belong to?"

"Not yet. No one's been reported missing lately."

"Well," said the lieutenant, "this could be a tough solve if the solution is acid and no one new is reported to be missing."

"Rick and I discussed that, LT."

The lieutenant paused. "Ferry Creek Dam. I haven't been up there in years. As I recall, it's beautiful around the dam."

"It is," said Patty. "When I was young, lots of us kids would ride our bikes up there and fish. We always caught a few."

The lieutenant smiled. "Was the guy who discovered the barrel with ODFW?"

"No, he was with the local fishermen's group. Volunteers oversee the smolt acclimation pen."

The lieutenant nodded. "Let me know what the doc says."

"Will do, LT."

Patty returned to her desk and filled Rick in about her conversation with the lieutenant. "You look like the cat that just ate the canary. I expect you're about to tell me what you have in mind for our new chief."

Rick leaned forward in his seat. "You know the psychic across town who advertises being able to communicate with the dead and predict the future?"

"Yes," Patty said, drawing out the middle of the word.

"I'm going to call her."

Patty had a puzzled look on her face. "Why?"

Rick smiled. "I'm going to call her, stop by, and pick up some brochures."

He paused while Patty continued to look puzzled.

She said, "I get the feeling you're trying to tell me something, but I don't get it. For what reason are you going to call a psychic, and what does it have to do with the chief?"

Rick couldn't help but laugh, thinking of what he was about to say. "I'll leave the brochures on my desk and pin one up on the department bulletin board."

A brief silence followed Rick's words, then Patty smiled. "That's hilarious! But do you think he'll get it?"

Rick shrugged. "I hope so. He's the one who wanted to know our secret to solving homicides."

"That's very good, Rick."

"I'm going to enjoy this as much now as when we used it with my captain in Boston."

CHAPTER 5

Thursday morning, Patty walked in with a bakery box. She sent a card around with a pen so that everyone could write out their birthday wish for Brad. The cake received some oohs and aahs as she removed it from the box and set it on the table. Rick had asked Brad's partner Pete to keep the birthday boy busy until eight-fifteen, then bring him into the break room. Officers and staff stepped into the room as time grew near for Brad to arrive. At the planned time, Patty heard the front door open and Pete suggesting that they get their coffee before getting on with the day's work. A great Happy Birthday cheer went up as Brad entered the room.

Hanging his head, and noticeably touched by the gesture, he nodded to several of the well-wishers. He turned to Pete. "Did you know about this?"

Pete laughed. "Oh, yeah. Who else is going to make sure you're here as planned? Want to give a speech?"

With that, another cheer went up from some. Others cried out, "No. It will go on for hours."

Patty cut a slice of cake for everyone while Brad read his card. Rick returned to his desk with his cake in one hand and coffee mug in the other. A short time later, Patty returned to her desk with cake and coffee. She noticed Rick's cake had already been eaten.

"Good?" she asked.

"Yeah. Chocolate. My favorite."

"I'll make a mental note of that," said Patty.

Rick looked at his watch. "We'd better head out for Medford if we want to be there when the doc looks at the bones found in the barrel."

Patty sipped on her coffee. "Did you confirm the time?"

"Yep. She figured one pm, right after her lunch."

Patty glanced at her phone. "It's a two-and-a-half-hour drive. If we leave now, we'll get to Medford about noon, giving us time for lunch before our meeting."

The detectives put their files away and their jackets on.

"You drive," said Patty, "and I'll share more history with you."

Rick picked up his keys from the desk. "Works for me."

Heading south on Highway 101, Rick drove about sixteen miles before turning east on Highway 197, a connecting route to Highway 199.

He passed by Jedediah Smith State Park. "This is sure a great location for a state park. People come from all over the country to experience the redwood trees that we enjoy year-round. I heard the other day that a woman stopped in at the Crissey Field Welcome Center and asked for directions to see the redwoods. The host at the Center let her know that she drove past them for several miles on her way into Curry County."

"Sounds like someone who doesn't know her trees," said Patty. "The next time we're on this route, I'll let you sit in the passenger seat. Then you can take in the scenery rather than having to concentrate on driving. The driver never really gets to enjoy the total view because of the hazards."

Rick agreed. "You mean the hairpin curves, the canyon, and Smith River on one side of us, and the rock wall on the other? They do make it difficult to take one's eyes off the road. I wouldn't mind enjoying the view, so don't hesitate to ask if you want to drive back."

Patty smiled. "I'll let you know. Once you've made the turn up here, I'll tell you about one of the small towns we'll drive through."

The turn onto the main east-west highway between the coast and Josephine County came quickly.

"Ready for that lesson?" asked Patty.

"Ready."

"Let's start with the town of Merlin. With a population of less than 1,800, it's one of the larger towns off of 199. The town had several names before Merlin, which is another name for the pigeon hawk. It was founded by the postmaster at the time. The first post office was established in 1885. In 1880 the Southern Pacific Railroad established the first Jump-Off Joe Station, named after Jump-Off Joe Creek. The name originated when a guy named Joseph fell off a rock near the creek. The locals named the area 'Jump Off Where Joe Fell,' a name they later shortened to 'Jump-Off Joe.'

"The other and more well-known river we'll come upon during our drive through Grants Pass is, of course, the Rogue. Early fur traders named it the River of the Rogues after the Shasta, Takelma, and Rogue River Athabaskan tribes who inhabited the area.

"In 1850 Rogue River country was the site of the first gold rush in Oregon, as well as the scene of the Rogue River wars between native people and white settlers. Years later, during the twentieth century, the river became what it is today, well known for salmon fishing and challenging white-water rafting."

"That is all very interesting, Patty. Once again, you never cease to amaze me with your knowledge of southern Oregon. I want to hear more about the Rogue River wars."

"I don't know a lot more, but I'll tell you what I've read. The Rogue River wars took place from 1855 and 1856. It was an armed conflict between the US Army, local militias, volunteers, and the Native American tribes. From what little I've read, there was blame on all sides.

"The interaction among the Indians and first European-American settlers traveling through the area was peaceful. That changed with the opening of the Oregon Trail and the gold rush in Northern California and later eastern Oregon. These events resulted in large groups of settlers and miners arriving in the area and consuming the natural resources upon which the Indians depended. The growing population of settlers was catching fish and cutting down forests. Once the killing started, it became a matter of revenge, first by one side and then the other. I've read accounts of the war from more than one viewpoint, and, like all wars, it came down to more than one group of people wanting the same area of land."

Rick was silent as Patty continued. "And, on that note, I'm going to leave your history lesson and think about where to start with the Barrel Bones Murder."

Rick glanced at Patty. "The case has an ID?"

"It does. I find it less cumbersome calling it the Barrel Bones Murder rather than the Ferry Creek Dam Murder. And we don't know yet if our victim was killed at the dam or someplace else. What do you think?"

"Yeah. I like it. I've told you about my Boston buddy, Chuck Spencer. Well, naming his cases was something that Chuck always did. My second thought is that we pull over here and eat lunch." Rick pulled into the restaurant parking lot.

A waitress seated the detectives and gave them each a menu. She then, at lightning speed, recited the specials for the day. "Do you need a minute to decide?"

Rick handed back his menu and looked at her name badge. "I don't need more time. What was the third special you mentioned?"

The waitress stared at the ceiling momentarily as though lining up the specials. "The third one was chicken-fried steak with hashbrowns and gravy."

"That's what I'll have, Sherry. Thank you."

Sherry's eyes got big. "Oh my gosh, that's amazing."

Rick looked at Patty and then up at Sherry. "What's amazing?"

"Well, you know. I mean, out of all the girls' names in this world, you guessed mine on the first try. You are just amazing."

Rick sat up straight and deeply inhaled, expanding his chest. He smiled at Patty. "Well, I guess I am." He turned back toward Sherry and smiled. "And I owe it to you for noticing, and for letting my boss, here, know too."

Before he could go on, Patty spoke to Sherry. "I'll have the chef salad." She then pointed. "You might want to straighten your name badge. It's sitting a bit crooked."

Sherry let out a little laugh. "Oh, thanks, but it always turns crooked."

She took Patty's menu. "One chef salad and one chicken-fried steak coming right up."

Rick continued to smile at Patty. "You know, it's good to be appreciated."

Patty closed her eyes and shook her head.

When Sherry returned to the table with the order, she spoke to Rick. "I figured it out, you know."

Rick looked up at her. "Figured what out?"

"I figured out how you knew my name. My name badge, right?"

Rick cleared his throat. "Well, Sherry, you got me. And I apologize if in any way I offended you by calling you by your name."

Sherry laughed. "Oh, no, you didn't offend me. I think it's pretty funny. As a matter of fact, I'm going to try that trick on my friend Sally. She's a waitress too."

Rick smiled. "Well, I'm glad I could lighten your day."

When Sherry left, Rick looked at Patty and shrugged. "What can I say?"

Patty smiled. "I can tell, having waitressed briefly in college, that she's the exception. Restaurant servers like, for instance, those who work for Patty at Blue Water Café and Lounge, have to be smart. They are slammed a good deal of the time and must take and deliver orders, all the while keeping a smile on their faces."

"I know. Just having a bit of fun. I've observed how hard they work when we eat lunch there. I couldn't do the job without mixing up orders or spilling coffee."

When the detectives arrived at the State Medical Examiner's building, the doc had spread the bones out on the table and placed them into the form of a human skeleton.

"Hi, Doc," said Patty. "Life treating you well?"

"I'm just as busy as ever, but busy can be good. As long as you keep finding bodies, I'll have a job. Hi, Rick."

"Hey, Doc. Good to know we contribute to your financial well-being."

Patty walked up beside the metal table. "Tell us what you know, Doc."

The doctor picked up a pointer. "I can tell you a few things about your victim. First, he was male. Second, the liquid in the drum was a solution consisting of both lye and water from the dam. You are fortunate the lid of the drum was not secured tightly. A solution comprised solely of lye would have disintegrated the body in a matter of hours. I'd estimate that the barrel went into the water very soon after the body was placed in the solution. If the body was folded into the lye directly after death and quickly dropped into the dam reservoir, you are probably looking at two to three days since your victim was killed. Hard to confirm a time of death if the deceased was killed days before being placed in the barrel."

Rick crossed his arms over his chest. "Why lye instead of acid, Doc?"

Before answering, the doc walked to a counter against one wall and drank from a coffee mug. A half-eaten sandwich lay on the plate next to where the mug had sat. "Lye is much easier than acid to obtain because strong acids are used in bombs. Their sales are tightly monitored. Sulfuric acid, for example, is also highly hazardous. It can cause third-degree burns and its fumes are dangerous to breathe. In addition to being easier to obtain, lye is cheaper and less dangerous to the person handling it."

"Handling lye sounds pretty simple," said Patty.

The doc emptied her coffee cup. "Lye has its own drawbacks. It is unique in that it must be heated before adding it to water. So you're looking for one or more people with the ability and accommodation to heat up enough lye to make a barrel full of solution."

"That should narrow down the possible suspects for us," said Rick. "Anything else?"

"Yes. I don't believe it was the lye that killed him." The doc directed the pointer to the sternum. "Though the lye has disintegrated a lot of the bone, there's a clear indentation here where a weapon went through and pierced the heart. If the solution had not been weakened by the influx of water, there would be little if anything left of the sternum. But this guy got lucky when the lid was not secured tightly on the drum."

Rick looked at the table. "Yeah, real lucky."

Patty looked closely at the notch in the sternum. "Any idea what was used?"

"Certainly not right now and possibly not at all due to the condition of the bone."

"Well, Doc, now we know how this victim was killed. Do you think you'll get any DNA off what's left of him?"

"No, this is one victim from which we're not going to find nuclear or mitochondrial DNA."

Patty exhaled loudly. "Well, thanks, Doc. We appreciate your working us into your schedule so quickly."

The doc smiled. "You both look totally bummed. But take heart, I'm about to make your day. This victim's luck just goes on and on."

The detectives waited in anticipation as the doc continued. "Take a good look at his left fibula."

Rick and Patty walked around the table observing the bone from both sides.

"What do you see?" asked the doc.

Rick pointed toward the bone. "There are holes in what appears to be a vertical pattern."

"You are correct, Detective Starker. Now, can either of you guess why?"

"Maybe," said Patty, "the victim could have had hardware attached to his fibula at some time. Maybe due to a break?"

Standing next to the counter, the doc held up a vertical stainless-steel plate. "This is how your victim will solve the mystery of his own identification. It's a Stryker Fibula."

The room was dead quiet, and then Rick laughed.

"I'm beginning to feel like this is a test, Doc. Enlighten us."

"Orthopedic surgical implants such as this have a serial number and company name engraved in them. I've already sent the number to Stryker. They'll have identification of your victim within the next forty-eight hours."

"Wow!" said Patty.

"In thirty years," said Rick, "I've never come across a case where implanted hardware was the only clue to identifying the victim. This is great!"

The doc smiled. "I'm sure the killer or killers didn't know this, or they'd have known the lye wouldn't destroy the stainless steel."

"I'm already enjoying the thought," said Rick, "of using this against them."

Patty agreed. "Yeah. It's going to shake up the courtroom."

"Now," said the doc, "I've got a question for you two. What kind of a person kills someone and then puts them into a barrel of lye?"

Patty spoke first. "Someone who wants to leave no evidence."

The doc nodded and smiled. "Guess our Mr. Lucky here has put one over on the killer and is having the last laugh."

CHAPTER 6

During the drive back to Brookings, the detectives discussed their "lucky" victim and how they'd soon know whose bones were in the barrel. The conversation then turned personal.

Patty looked out the window. "It's supposed to rain this weekend. What do you want to do?"

"Guess I hadn't thought that far ahead. How about we watch a movie we haven't seen?"

Patty looked out the window. "I'd like that. Got anything in mind?"

"Well, how about *Mystery Road*? We enjoyed the series and would probably like the movie too."

"Good choice. I'll bring the popcorn."

After a few minutes of silence, Patty turned again to Rick. "Have you been to the Brookings Azalea Festival Art Show?"

"I don't think so. Where is it?"

"It takes place at Azalea Middle School. It's this weekend. I'd like to go, and if you come with me, we'd have time for the art show before watching *Mystery Road*."

Rick looked over at Patty. "You're not trying to induct me into the realm of the art world, are you?"

Patty smiled. "Does it matter?"

"Not as long as you won't be disappointed if I'm not ready to take up painting after the show."

Patty reached over and touched Rick's arm. "I won't."

The moment was interrupted by the ringtone of Patty's phone. "It's Becky," she said to Rick and took the call.

"Hi, Becky."

"Hey, Mom. This a good time to talk?"

"It is, Bec, but Rick and I are travelling 199 back to Brookings. I'll call back from the office if I lose you."

"No problem, Mom. You and Rick in Medford to see the doc?"

"We were."

"Anyone I know?"

"Probably not. You'll read in the paper that we've got bones."

"Well, you and Rick will figure it out."

"Thanks, Bec. How are things going with you?"

"Pretty well. I'm enjoying teaching part-time, but I'm not sure this is where I want to end up. I took an online exam this morning in psychology, and I think I aced it."

"That's great, Bec! I'm pleased you called to let me know."

"Well, that's not the only reason for the call. I met a guy."

"Oh? Is this someone you want to know better?"

"It is, Mom. He's asked me to go out to dinner with him on Saturday."

"That's a nice start, Bec. What's his name and how did you meet him? Is he in one of your classes?"

"His name is Owen Reed and he's in my psych class."

"Oh," said Patty. "What degree is he working toward?"

"He's finishing up a double degree in law and psychology. He'll take the bar next year."

"That's a good combination. If he plans to litigate, he can use his knowledge of psychology to appeal to the jury."

"That's the idea, Mom. He wants to work for the DA."

"Have you talked to Owen about your goals?"

Becky laughed. "You mean about how I keep changing them?"

"There's nothing wrong, Bec, with changing your major. Life is easier if you work in a field you enjoy. Pick a major and know that you don't have to spend a lifetime in that field. You've done well along those lines already by getting your teaching certification and using it part-time while you continue to study."

"I get that, Mom. You've mentioned it before, and it's good to be reminded. I am thinking in a different direction now."

Patty began to respond when the connection dropped. She returned her phone to her purse and looked over at Rick.

He glanced her way. "Becky doing okay?"

"She seems to be doing okay. She has a new boyfriend and may be changing her major, again."

"What is she interested in now?"

"The connection dropped before she could tell me. I'll call her back from the office."

A short time later, Rick pulled into the department parking lot. "After driving five hours, I need a cup of coffee and whatever sweet is in the break room. Do you want something?"

"No, thanks, I'm fine."

Back at her desk, Patty called her daughter and continued their conversation. After the call, Patty got Rick's attention. "Ready to hear the rest of the news from Bec?"

Rick took a bite of cookie and nodded.

"Becky's doing fine, in part because she has a new boyfriend. He's majoring in both law and psychology, and will take the bar next year."

Rick picked up his pen. "Yeah? What's his name?"

"Owen Reed. He's in her psych class. The other news she had was pretty much what it's been for a while. She's still not sure she wants to stick with teaching. This will be her fourth time to change her major. I guess I shouldn't be concerned because she is supporting herself while she continues her schooling. It's just that I'd like to know that she's happy with her work. What do you think about her uncertainty?"

"Well, like you, Patty, I chose law enforcement early and stayed with it.

I've never regretted my choice. With the way things are out there today in many communities, I might have second thoughts if I were a young person looking for the same career."

"I've thought about that too, Rick. Can't say I'd want Becky to become a cop right now. The last few years have been rough on law enforcement."

Rick sighed. "Becky needs a little more time to decide what will make her happy. She's a responsible person and is just being cautious. She's way ahead of many young people in that she is supporting herself. You've done a great job, Patty."

"Thanks, Rick. I'm very proud of her."

Rick's cell phone lit up, ending the conversation. He glanced at caller ID. "I need to get this. Chuck Spencer! Great to hear from you."

Patty could just make out what the caller was saying. "Good to be talking with you, Rick. "I've got some time off and thought I'd head for the Oregon coast. You got an extra bed?"

"I sure do, Chuck. It will be great seeing you. I've mentioned you to my partner, and I know she'll be pleased to meet the man who is somewhat of a legend in Boston."

"That's a heavy load for me to carry. I was just good at my job."

"*Was* good? You've retired?"

"Last month. I had thirty-one years on the job with the last fifteen in SWAT. I figured it was someone else's turn. I'm travelling across the country to see family and friends. The way you've described the southern Oregon coast, I might even buy a place out there to hang my hat during the summer."

"That would be great, Chuck. When do you plan on arriving?"

"Next Wednesday, if that works for you."

"It does. We'll see you Wednesday. Call when you have an ETA."

Patty eagerly waited for Rick to talk about his call. "I know that was your good friend, Chuck. I could hear some of the conversation, so I know he's visiting. This week?"

Rick smiled. "Yeah. He'll arrive Wednesday. He's retired and travelling across the country. He's also considering buying something out here so that he can spend more time on the coast. Chuck is a great guy. You'll like him."

"You've mentioned how effective he was in Boston. I'm looking forward to hearing some of his stories."

"I'm sure he'll tell a few. The psychic idea we played on the captain in Boston was Chuck's idea. His way of solving crimes was amazing. It's like he had a sixth sense. And the manner in which he'd observe a crime scene became part of his trademark. When Chuck arrived at the scene, he'd walk in slowly and find a place where he could sit down without interfering with the evidence. Sometimes that was on a chair against the wall. Another time, it might be on the arm of a couch. Then he'd just carefully take in what he could see throughout the room. And, nine times out of ten, he'd see something that became a clue in solving the case."

"Do you remember one of those successful cases?"

"I do. But before I tell you about it, I just remembered one other trait of Chuck's that is important to visualize. Chuck likes knives. He has some beautiful collector knives including a few by Half Face Blades and several different types of knives that make a clicking sound when manipulated. One of the knives he always carried is a balisong. When he sat down in a room to look for clues in a crime, he'd pull out his balisong and begin flipping it."

Patty interrupted, "I've never heard of someone in law enforcement doing that at a crime scene. Why did he?"

"That," Rick said, "is something you'll have to ask Chuck. Continuing on with the case, we had someone call reporting a missing person. The mother said that her sixteen-year-old daughter had run away. We knew that a girl's body had been discovered earlier that day with no ID on her. The mother of the runaway was asked to come in and view the body to determine if it was her daughter. It was. Our runaway was now a possible homicide.

"Chuck was a detective at the time and got the call to respond to the girl's home. He entered the home, sat down on a chair, and began carefully looking at everything in the room, all the while flipping his balisong. He spotted a cell phone on the couch partially tucked between two cushions. Under the couch he found a girl's purse. He looked inside and found the deceased's driver's license. He approached the mother and confirmed that both the phone and the purse were her daughter's. What sixteen-year-old leaves home voluntarily without her cell phone and purse? Turned out the mother was the stepmother, who'd married the girl's father only two years prior. She was jealous of the attention her new husband gave to his daughter and hired someone to take care of her problem."

"That was a quick solve. Did the stepmother talk?"

"She did, and now enjoys the hospitality of a Massachusetts women's correctional facility. Switching gears, want to plan on the three of us having dinner Wednesday?"

"That would be great."

Patty's phone rang. "It's the doc." She picked up. "Hey, Doc. Got something for us?"

"Just called to let you know that it could take an extra day for us to get the identity of your victim. Computer problems coupled with a sick employee are causing a bit of a delay. I'll let you know as soon as I do."

"Thanks, Doc. Guess we were being too optimistic."

"Hmmm. Got to remember, Patty, it's always something. You're both welcome."

The call ended as there was a knock at the office door.

"Hey, Brad," said Patty. "What's up?"

"Two things. Got a minute?"

Patty looked at Rick and then back to Brad. "We do."

"First, I want to thank you both for the card and cake."

"You're welcome," said Patty. "What's the second thing?"

"It's about a report. A woman called in earlier today saying she's concerned about her younger brother. Says he would call once a week to check on her while she's undergoing cancer treatment. She said he missed his call this week and hasn't returned the messages she's left on his home or work phone." Brad handed a piece of paper to Patty. "There's her name and contact information. I'm wondering if it could be connected to the Barrel Bones case?"

"Could be," said Patty. "We may need you and Pete to do some neighborhood canvassing for us."

"At your service. Just point us in the right direction."

Patty smiled. "Thanks, Brad. We'll make a few initial calls and let you know."

Patty called the number in Brad's note. It was answered on the second ring. "Hello?"

"Hello. This is Detective O'Toole calling for Cindi Browning."

"This is Cindi."

"Miss Browning, before we continue, I want to let you know that I've got you on speaker phone so that my partner, Detective Starker, can participate in the conversation. We've been told you called into the station today."

"That's correct, Detective. I am worried that something has happened to my brother Grant."

"Why do you think something's happened to your brother?"

"I'm worried because he didn't call last week. You see, I have cancer, stage 4. My husband died three years ago, and I have no children. I have no other siblings, so that left Grant to care for me. Since he lives in Oregon and I'm eight hours away in California, his care for months now has been a weekly phone call, until last week."

"Is it possible that he's off taking a vacation and just forgot to call?"

"No. He'd have told me if he was going to be away, and his checking on me isn't something he'd forget. He's a very responsible guy."

"What's your brother's name?"

"Grant Wellingham."

"What about a girlfriend?" Rick asked. "Some girls can make a guy a little forgetful."

"I hear what you're suggesting, Detective, but Grant is going through a very difficult divorce. Very difficult. He won't be looking for another relationship anytime soon."

Patty looked up from her notes. "What his wife's or soon-to-be ex-wife's name?"

"Her name is Crystal Lowe Wellingham. She owns the CLW Real Estate firm in Brookings."

"Do you know why Crystal and your brother are divorcing?"

"Well, it seems that after seven years and two kids they grew tired of each other. I'm surprised they've stayed married this long."

"Why's that?" asked Patty.

"Well, I wouldn't say this if it weren't for my concern about Grant. She doesn't care about anything except money. She was a realtor for another firm when they met and then married. She decided she wanted her own real estate firm, and she wanted it downtown on your main street. She didn't have the money, so they used Grant's savings to sign a long-term lease and completely refurbish the inside of the space. Have you ever been in the lobby of her firm?"

"No," said Patty. "Can't say that I have."

"Well, it's like a palace. Very expensive furnishings. And my brother paid for it all. It made no difference how much he gave her because she always wanted more. And he was constantly apologizing."

"Apologizing?" Patty asked. "For what?"

"Anything and everything. The last time I was with them both, about a year ago, she blurted out that she didn't feel good and that he should have come home early from work. He told her that he didn't know she was unwell because she hadn't said anything about it. Her response to him was that he should have known what she was feeling. Every time I was with them at an event, he was apologizing to her for not knowing what she was thinking or feeling."

"I see," said Patty. "Do you know if she ever hit him?"

"No. She'd never do something that would leave a mark others might see. But it was clear she didn't love him. I don't think she ever did."

Rick cleared his throat. "When did they start their divorce?"

"Oh, it must have been about two years ago."

"Two years. Why do you suppose it's taking so long?"

"To be honest, I just don't know. My understanding is that he's willing to give her most of their assets. I don't know what is holding it up. Maybe you can talk with his attorney."

"We'll do that," said Patty. "Do you have the attorney's contact information, Miss Browning?"

"Yes, I do. I'm widowed, so it's Ms. Browning. But, please, call me Cindi. I'll email the attorney's name and phone number."

"Okay, Cindi. We may need to talk with you again. Call if you think of anything else that might help us to find him, and let us know if your brother contacts you.”

“Well,” Patty said to Rick, “she didn’t ask if we knew of any deaths, but she’ll soon read about the bones. I expect she’ll call back when the discovery is published. She’s already emailed the attorney information. I’ll call and set up an appointment for tomorrow.”

Patty’s call to the attorney was brief. She glanced at her watch and then at Rick. “We have a nine-thirty appointment tomorrow with attorney Harvey Starr at a downtown firm. Maybe we’ll learn if there was a reason for Grant Wellingham to disappear. I’ll set up an appointment to meet with Crystal after we see Starr. It’s getting late. Want to call it a day?”

Rick stood and put on his jacket. “That works for me.” He walked up to Patty and gently kissed her. “See you in the morning.”

Patty reached out her hand and touched Rick’s cheek. “Good night, Rick.”

CHAPTER 7

It was early when Kevin arrived at work. He started the morning as always, looking over his calendar for notes on the day's appointments. His concentration was interrupted by the vibration of his cell phone indicating a call.

"This is Kevin. Yes, that is my listing, and it is still available. What's your name? Do you live locally? Is it you and your wife who are looking? Let me check my schedule. I can meet you in my office this afternoon at either one or four-thirty. Oh, I see. When do you expect to be here? Wednesday. Does one-thirty work for you? Okay. Wednesday at one-thirty it is. Is this the best phone number for me to reach you at in the event we need to change our plans? Very good. I'll text you my office address."

CHAPTER 8

Patty walked into the office and found Rick at his desk. "Good morning. Been here long?"

"Yeah, I woke up at four thinking about this missing-person case and figured I'd come in and prepare some questions for the soon-to-be ex-wife." Rick pointed to the white bakery bag on his desk. "There's one in there for you if you're interested."

Patty walked around the desk and peeked into the bag. She pulled out a doughnut. "Chocolate Old-Fashioned. My favorite. How did you know?"

"I must be psychic," said Rick.

Patty smiled. "Must be."

"Speaking of psychics, I see our local one this afternoon. The brochures will go up after that."

Patty swallowed a bit of her doughnut. "This is either going to give the chief a good laugh or get us suspended."

Rick smiled. "Yeah, but it will be worth it."

Patty nodded and sipped on her coffee. "Back to the case. How much do you think the attorney will tell us?"

Rick shrugged. "Not a lot, unless he too has been trying to reach his client with no response."

"I agree. I'll call and set up the appointment with the wife."

Patty brought up Crystal's name and number on her phone, hit the call button, and heard the call being picked up on the first ring.

"Good morning. This is Crystal."

"Crystal, this is Detective O'Toole with the Brookings Police Department. We've received a call about your husband and need to ask a few questions. Is there a time this afternoon when my partner, Detective Starker, and I can meet with you at your office or here at ours?"

"You have questions about Grant? Why?"

"I'd rather not hold this conversation over the phone. Can you meet us at eleven-thirty?"

"Yes. I'll be here at my office."

"We'll see you then."

Patty ended the call and put the appointment time into her phone. "Grant could be our Barrel Bones victim. Hard to think of a disgruntled ex-wife going to such lengths to get rid of her husband. Maybe he was caught up in some drug war."

Rick stood up with his empty coffee mug. "That was a common occurrence in Boston. Not so much here, but a possibility." He pointed to Patty's coffee. "I'm going for a refill. Want one?"

Patty held up her cup. "Thanks."

At nine-thirty, the detectives sat in the law office of Harvey Starr. Rick and Patty carefully looked around the room.

Rick asked, "Is this a large law firm?"

Harvey nodded. "We have a dozen attorneys with practices affiliated with several areas of law."

"A Chris Hawthorne blown-glass vase and an office with an ocean view," said Rick. "You must be doing pretty well."

Harvey looked at the vase before responding. "I do okay." He looked back at Rick. "You seem to know your artists."

"Just that one," Rick said. "I enjoy his Port Orford gallery."

Harvey nodded. "Well, you didn't come here to assess the success of my business. My secretary said you wanted to ask questions about one of my clients.

You know that I can't divulge anything that's confidential, so what can I do for you?"

Patty responded. "We're here to ask a few questions about your client, Grant Wellingham. When is the last time you met or spoke with him?"

Harvey hit a button on his desk phone, and his secretary answered. "Maria, when was Mr. Wellingham's last appointment?" Following a brief pause, Maria gave the requested appointment date. Harvey looked at Patty. "He was here about three weeks ago."

"Have you tried reaching him on the phone since that appointment?"

Harvey sat back in his chair. "As a matter of fact, I have. Three days ago, I left a message asking him to call me."

"Is that unusual?" asked Patty. "For him not to call you back?"

"Now that I think about it, Detective, yes. It is. Grant generally gets back to me within a day or two, depending upon his work."

Rick looked up from his notes. "What kind of work is that?"

"Grant's in construction. He's a contractor. Your questions have me concerned. Has something happened to him?"

"That's what we're trying find out," said Patty. "If he'd taken a sudden vacation, would he necessarily have told you he was leaving?"

Harvey paused to think about the question. "No, he probably would not have told me he was leaving, but that doesn't mean he wouldn't have returned my call."

"Has Grant ever spoken about anyone who'd want to hurt him?"

Harvey looked across the room and then answered the question. "Hurt him? He's never mentioned anyone to me that he feared."

"What about the divorce?" asked Rick. "Is it amicable? Contentious?"

Harvey paused again. "Now you're getting into an area of confidentiality."

Patty leaned forward. "Really? Your client seems to have gone missing, and it's our job to look at every possible reason for his absence. I'm not asking you to give us detailed reasons for his divorce, but I do need to know whether we should have reason to suspect that he's been kidnapped or hurt by someone who is angry with him."

Harvey fidgeted in his chair. "The divorce is very contentious."

Patty glanced at Rick and they both stood up. Patty looked toward Harvey. "Thank you." She turned to leave, stopped, and turned back toward the attorney. "One last question. Has your client mentioned anything about his sister, Cindi Browning?"

"Yes. I put Grant's trust together for him. Cindi is his co-trustee with me. The trust was made before Cindi became ill. I believe he calls her weekly."

"Thanks again," said Patty.

The detectives walked out of the law office and down the street to Rick's car.

"It will be interesting to learn how the wife describes their divorce," Rick said.

Patty opened the passenger door. "It's good we know the answer to that question before asking her."

Patty walked into the lobby of CLW Real Estate and looked up. "Wow, the lobby is just as Cindi described. This does look a bit palatial."

"Yeah," Rick agreed. "It needs a doorman to top it off."

A young woman at the front desk greeted the detectives. "Can I help you?"

Patty smiled. "We're here to see Crystal Wellingham."

"Oh, well, Crystal isn't here at the moment. Do you have an appointment?"

"We do," said Patty.

"Well, I'm sure she'll be coming in any minute." She pointed toward the couch. "Would you like to sit down?"

The front door opened and a smartly-dressed woman walked in.

"Well, here she is now."

The detectives turned to find Crystal Wellingham walking into the room with her hand outstretched toward Rick. "Detectives, I'm sorry to be a little late. The tourist season has started, resulting in traffic far heavier than usual."

Rick shook Crystal's hand. She didn't extend it toward Patty, nor did Patty welcome a handshake from Crystal. "Please, come into my office."

Crystal's office décor was an extension of the lobby. Three glass jellyfish hung from the ceiling. The young woman who greeted them upon arrival walked in and set down a cup of coffee on Crystal's desk. She turned toward Patty and Rick. "May I get you something?"

"No, thank you," said Patty.

The greeter left and Crystal smiled. "You said you have some questions."

"We're here," said Patty, "to ask about your husband, Grant." She waited for a response.

"Grant? Why are you asking me about Grant? I mean he is my husband; however, we are in the process of a divorce. We no longer live together and have very little to do with each other."

Patty continued. "When is the last time you saw or heard from him?"

Crystal brought the calendar up on her phone and brushed through the pages. "We last saw each other about twelve days ago, when he took the kids for the weekend."

"And you haven't spoken with him or seen each other since then?"

Crystal looked at her phone again. "No. Anything we have to say regarding our divorce is handled through our attorneys. Why do you ask? Is Grant in trouble with the law?"

Patty ignored the question. "Would you say that your divorce is amicable?"

Crystal nodded. "Oh, yes. We're divorcing because we've grown apart. Neither of us has any interest in punishing the other. We want things to go smoothly for the kids. I'd say it's been very polite and friendly."

Patty glanced at Rick, and he addressed the broker.

"You said twelve days since you've seen your husband, and that was to give him the kids for a weekend. How often does Grant see his children?"

Crystal looked down on the top of her desk and moved a glass paperweight around in a circle. "Grant is a good father, but he works long hours and just can't see the kids every weekend. I have a nanny at my home to care for the children since I, too, work long hours."

"I see," said Rick. "Has Grant ever taken off for a week or two without coordinating the kids' schedule with you?"

Crystal played again with the paperweight. "Look, Detectives, I've answered several questions now, and you still haven't told me why you're here. Is Grant in some kind of trouble?"

Patty looked at Rick and nodded. Then she turned to Crystal. "Grant hasn't been in contact with his sister for more than a week. She called Grant's employer and found that he hasn't been in to work either during that time." She sat silently, waiting for Crystal's reaction. The otherwise composed woman sat forward with her hands held tight together on top of the desk.

"Well, that's unexpected. He and Cindi were pretty close. Seems you've spoken with his sister. I hope nothing's happened to him. Do you have any idea as to why he's missing?"

Patty responded quietly, "No, we don't."

Rick looked at Crystal and spoke very deliberately. "You said, 'were.' Why not 'are'?"

Crystal was clearly surprised by Rick's question and, at first, seemed not to know how to answer. "What do you mean?"

"You said that Grant and his sister 'were' pretty close. Why speak of that relationship in the past tense?"

Crystal squirmed in her chair. "I just made a mistake is all. I meant to say that they are very close. Your questions have just made me nervous about the possibility that something bad has happened to Grant."

Rick nodded.

Patty put her business card on the desk. "Give me a call if you think of anything else we should know."

"Oh, I will," Crystal said, picking up the card. "I'll call if I hear anything."

After returning to their office, Patty opened the discussion. "What do you think?"

Rick hung his jacket on the back of his chair and sat down. "Based upon her comments, we can be reasonably sure she lied about how well she and Grant got along. So I have to ask myself why. Why wouldn't she tell us the truth about their contentious relationship? And, if she's lied to us about that, why should we believe anything else she said?"

Patty tapped her pencil on the desk. "Let's talk with Grant's boss. Ask him about the tone of the relationship. Surely Grant talked at work about his divorce."

Rick nodded and looked at his watch. "How about we interview him and then wrap up the day with a drink at Dewy's? There's a chance he's not yet left work if we go now."

"Good plan," said Patty.

Grant's boss was at his desk working on a bid when Patty and Rick walked in.

"Mr. Brown?" Patty asked.

"That's right. How can I help you?"

Patty showed her shield. "We're Detectives O'Toole and Starker. We'd like to ask a few questions about Grant Wellingham."

"I'm not in much of a mood right now to talk about Grant. He's left me in a mess."

"What kind of a mess?"

"He was foreman on a house we're building. The owner waited three months until the end of our rainy season, and then, after only two weeks on the job, Grant took off."

Rick looked at his notepad. "You said he was foreman. Why past tense?"

Brown's face turned a slight shade of red. "Because he can't just walk away from a job and expect to return anytime he wants and step back into his position. I've put someone else on the job. I'm angry but I'm also puzzled."

"Puzzled?" asked Patty.

"Yeah. Grant's a smart guy and a very good contractor. I know he's going through a divorce, but he hadn't let it interfere with his job until now. I'm guessing he's in some kind of trouble with the law since the two of you are here. Care to fill me in?"

"He's not," said Patty, "in any trouble that we know of. His sister called us worried that something's happened to him."

Brown sat back in his chair. "That the one who has cancer?"

"Yes," said Patty. "You know her?"

"I've never met her. Grant's told me about her. She helped his mother raise him when Grant's father left. His sister means a lot to him. If she's worried, there must be a reason why."

Rick took notes while Patty continued the questioning.

"Tell us what you know about his relationship with his wife."

Brown took a pack of gum from the center drawer of his desk. "Haven't smoked for 78 days. Doc says I need to quit." He extended his arm toward the detectives. "Gum?" he asked.

Patty responded, "No, thanks." Rick moved his head to indicate he wasn't interested.

"Grant and his wife fight all of the time."

"What about?" asked Patty.

"Anything and everything. They have for the two years I've known them. I feel sorry for their kids. This divorce should have been wrapped up months ago, but they've each been asking for something the other doesn't want to give."

"Like what?" asked Patty.

"Well, as I understand it, she wants both houses, and he wants half of her business."

"Both houses?" Patty asked.

"Yeah. They own the big one they live in, or that she now lives in with the kids since he spent his nights in a room I have in the back. Their winter home is in Arizona. The last time he spoke to me about their negotiating, he said she could have the main residence and half the proceeds from the sale of the Arizona house. She evidently will not give in to his request for half her business, and he's holding out. Says he bankrolled it and wants his share of the success." Brown sat up and leaned forward against his desk. "You know, I've been married to the same woman for thirty-four years. If she demanded a divorce, I'd take enough to live on and let her have the rest just to get away from the pain." He looked at Rick. "I just don't get it."

Patty gave her card to Mr. Brown. "You mentioned that Grant stayed in a back room. Does that include a bathroom? Would he have a toothbrush here?"

"Yeah, there is a bathroom. I haven't cleared his stuff out. I'll see if he left one."

Brown returned to the office with Grant's toothbrush. "Leaving his toothbrush here suggests he did not leave on a planned trip. Now I am concerned."

Patty put the toothbrush into a plastic evidence bag. "If you hear from Grant or from anyone who knows where he is, give us a call."

"I'll do that, Detective. I hope nothing bad has happened to him. This is the first time he's let me down, otherwise he's been a dependable guy."

Patty and Rick climbed back into Rick's unmarked car. He started the engine. "Ready for that drink?"

"Very," said Patty. "He mentioned an Arizona house. We need to get the address and ask the locals to check it out. Make sure Grant's not holed up there. I'll send his toothbrush to the lab."

Rick pulled into the department parking lot. "That can go on our agenda for tomorrow. Let's leave the unmarked and take my car to Dewy's."

Dewy's was crowded. Rick looked around the room for an empty table. "Tables are taken, but there are a few seats at the bar."

Patty nodded. "I see two seats together."

Patty sat down and hung her purse under the bar. "I recognize a few cops from Crescent City PD."

Rick took the other stool. "Yeah, I saw them too. Always good to have a safe place to hang out. Would you like a Chardonnay?"

"Thanks."

The bartender set napkins down in front of Patty and Rick. "How's it going, Detectives?"

"Busy," said Patty. "Looks like you are too."

One of the barmaids placed her tray on the bar with an order for several drinks.

Rick ordered. "She'll have a Chardonnay and I'll take a Coke. No ice."

The bartender walked away and began filling the order for several drinks at once. The guy sitting on the stool next to Patty was working on a beer and began talking to her. "Maybe you can explain something to me."

Patty glanced at Rick and then turned toward the guy. "Do I know you?"

"No. I just thought you might be able to help. I'm in a bad way all because of a woman. And I'm here to drown my sorrows."

Patty looked back at Rick, who could hear the conversation. He shrugged. Patty turned to the guy on the other side of her. "Well, I'm sorry you're in a bad way. Might want to think about taking a cab home."

The guy ignored the comment. "I was in love, you see, with a beautiful woman I met on the internet. She had auburn hair and baby blue eyes. We exchanged photos and talked every day. She was from Sweden and was prettier than anything I'd ever seen. Like one of those dolls, you know, with a ceramic head. No, not ceramic. I can't remember what it's called."

"Porcelain?" asked Patty.

"Yeah, that's it. Anyway, we fell in love and were going to get married. Had a date set and everything. All we needed was for her to fly out here. So I sent her the money for a one-way plane ticket."

The bartender walked over and set Patty's wine and Rick's Coke on the bar. He leaned toward the detectives. "What you need to know is that this is his third attempt at an overseas bride. He'll keep trying until he goes broke."

Rick shook his head, and Patty turned back to the forlorn drinker. "So you sent the money."

The dejected seeker of a bride looked surprised. "Of course I sent her the money. We were in love."

"If you sent her the money, why isn't she with you?"

The expression on the man's face now looked lost. "She turned out to be a Russian man. It was all a trick. Can you believe anyone would be so cruel?"

"Well," said Patty, "I'm sorry that happened to you. It seems that the internet might not be the best place for you to find a bride."

The forlorn man looked with surprise at Patty. "But it works. My neighbor found her husband on the internet. And after last night, I might not have to look any further."

Patty glanced up at the bartender, who was standing nearby. He shrugged with an I-told-you-so look. The man on the bar stool waited for Patty's response.

"Really?"

"That's right. Another beautiful woman, Anika, hooked up with me last night. I told her what happened, and she was very kind and sympathetic. I told her about the others, too. She was as shocked as I was. She wants to meet me. I'm just now realizing that I need a kind woman like her." The man slipped off the bar stool. "I'll go home. She may want to talk some more. She could be the one."

The bartender paused in front of the man and put the guy's bill down. He glanced again at Patty and Rick. The man paid his bill and Rick stopped him before he left.

"What's the name of the website you're using?"

The man told Rick and left.

Patty rolled her eyes and looked at Rick. "And people wonder why these scams are so common."

"Yeah," said Rick. "I ran into a lot of that while working in Boston. The women involved are not always voluntary participants. I'll give the website address to a friend back there who still works vice."

CHAPTER 9

The following day, Patty went to lunch with her mother as planned. She walked into the restaurant and saw Maggie sitting at a window table.

"Hi, Mom."

"Hello, dear. It's good to see you."

"Good to see you too, Mom. How's your day going so far?"

"Well, I got up today. That's always a good start. I went to the gym and walked on the treadmill for thirty minutes this morning. Then I returned home, took a shower, and dressed for lunch with you."

"I'm pleased you could fit me in to your calendar, Mom. You lead a pretty busy life. How are you relative to having lost Bill in the past year?"

"I'm managing, Patty. It isn't easy being alone again, but having lost your dad, I knew what to expect after losing Bill. It's not the same, but the grieving process has some similarities. I know that pain like I'm experiencing is something I must go through, and that it is a result of dearly loving someone."

"He was a great partner to you, wasn't he?"

"Yes, Patty. He was very good to me, and for me. Bill brought a lot of joy into my life."

"Mom, I'm sorry you have to go through another loss."

"Thank you, Patty. But loss is part of life. It's just a matter of timing. Some go far too soon. I'm fortunate to be living this long. Death of a loved one does make you much more aware of how you spend each day. I'm trying to make each one count. Like having lunch with my daughter."

Patty reached into her purse, took out a tissue, and dabbed the corners of her eyes. She reached out and took hold of her mother's hand. "I love you, Mom."

Maggie smiled. "You, Patty, are a wonderful daughter. Now, let me tell you about an exchange I had with a friend last week. I saw my friend Carol down at the port in the Hip-Nautic Gifts store." She laughed.

"What's so funny?"

"I hadn't thought of it until just now. The store building for Hip-Nautic Gifts used to be the Voodoo Bar."

Patty smiled. "Sort of an exchange of businesses with a suggested supernatural name."

"Yeah. Have you been there?"

Patty nodded. "That's where I bought my Brookings sweatshirt. It's a fun shop."

"Well, I told Carol that I'd spent the prior weekend volunteering at the Oregon Wine and Cheese Festival. I told her it kept me so busy that I was taking orders for six hours straight without a break. Well, Carol reacted with a surprised look and said, 'I'm impressed.' Then she bent at the waist and moved her arms up and down as though honoring someone. It took me a moment to figure out to what she was honoring me about, and then we both had a good laugh."

Patty paused before speaking. "I'm not getting it, Mom. What was so great about you going for six hours without a break?"

Maggie laughed. "Oh, dear. You're not old enough, Patty, but for some women my age, working for six hours without using the bathroom is a bit of a feat. I was sitting most of the time, which helped with my endurance."

"Oh," said Patty. "I feel a little dense. I guess I've now been forewarned about what's to come."

"Yes, but you've got many more years before you'll run into problems. So don't worry about it."

"Thanks for the reassurance. Our waitress is on her way over. Ready to order?"

* * *

Patty returned from lunch and joined Rick in their office.

He looked up from his writing. "How's your mom?"

"She's doing okay. I realize as I get older how much I admire her strength."

"I hope that you told her that."

Patty sat down at her desk. "Not in so many words, but I will the next time I see her." She opened the top drawer of her desk and took out a yellow legal pad. "Let's go through what we've got so far."

Rick opened the file on his desk. "All we have now is a probable missing-person case."

Patty added, "And a barrel of bones we've not yet identified."

Rick tapped his pencil on the file. "We've spoken with the missing person's sister, boss, and soon-to-be ex-wife, and concur that the wife lied to us about her relationship with the missing person."

"The question," Patty offered, "is why? Why did she lie?"

Rick responded, "She doesn't want us to know how dysfunctional her marriage is, or she doesn't want us to consider her as a suspect in her husband's disappearance."

Patty stopped writing. "I'm thinking it's the latter, but how and what did she do?"

"Or," said Rick, "is this a scam in which they are both involved? Is there life insurance to be collected if he's not found?"

"Let's find out," said Patty. "Continuing on, we know that the bones are those of a male who probably died within the past week to ten days."

"And was stabbed," said Rick, "before being stuffed into a drum of lye."

Patty made another note and read it to Rick. "The killer knew how to remove all identifying evidence from the victim, what type of weapon to use, and what kind of solution disintegrates flesh and bone. This was a carefully planned murder. One person could not have stuffed the man in the barrel, filled it with liquid, sealed it, and rolled it into the water."

Rick nodded. "I agree. I'm guessing there are two or three people involved."

Patty stopped writing. "So if our barrel bones victim is the missing Grant Wellingham, who's your number-one suspect?"

Rick paused before giving a response. "Based upon the interviews we've done thus far, I'd say it's the wife. And you?'

"I agree, Rick. Lying to us put her in the frame for the murder. Let's visit Ms. Crystal again. Find out the name of her life insurance agent, the address of the Arizona property, and go over again the relationship she has or had with Grant. Changing subjects, Chuck arrives tomorrow. Has he given you an ETA?"

"When I spoke with him yesterday, his plan was to arrive in Brookings about one-thirty and meet us here about three. He's got an appointment with a real estate agent upon arrival."

"That's good," said Patty. "I'll schedule our appointment with Crystal before one tomorrow."

Rick nodded. Patty tapped Crystal's phone number into her cell phone. The call was answered after the first ring. "Crystal here."

"Ms. Wellingham, this is Detective O'Toole. Detective Starker and I have a few more questions and would like to meet with you tomorrow morning. Would nine or eleven be better?"

Crystal laughed. "You sound like a salesman, Detective. Nine will be fine. I'll be in my office."

"We'll see you then," said Patty. Rick input the appointment information into his phone.

* * *

At nine the following morning, the detectives entered the CLW Real Estate office and were greeted again by a receptionist eager to please.

"Good morning, Detectives. Crystal is expecting you. Please have a seat and I'll let her know you're here."

Patty and Rick remained standing as the receptionist quickly let it be known to Crystal that her visitors had arrived. The impeccably-dressed woman walked into the room.

"Good morning, Detectives."

"Good morning. We appreciate your answering a few more of our questions."

"No problem. If Grant is in trouble, I want to do everything I can to help. Let's go back to my office."

Once they were all seated, Rick began the questioning. "We've spoken to your husband's sister, his boss, and his attorney. Their description of your marriage doesn't jibe with yours. They all maintain that the relationship you have with your husband is quite contentious. How do you explain the difference in opinion?"

Crystal shifted in her chair and played with her paperweight. As she struggled to answer, she looked up and to the right, a movement many consider an indication of lying. "I guess I did fudge a bit. It's not easy telling someone that your spouse is a greedy person. So, yes, we are not the perfect couple. Is there something else you wanted to ask me?"

Patty glanced at Rick. He leaned forward. "Why won't you split the business with him? It's our understanding that he bankrolled you, and half the business is all he wants to finalize the divorce."

Crystal's smile faded quickly. She squinted her eyes and spoke through gritted teeth. "I don't understand why that's any of your business. But if you must know, he may have helped me in the beginning, but it's been my labor and skill that made me successful. I'd have done okay without his money. It just would have taken a little longer. I built this business and I'm keeping all of it."

Patty spoke quietly. "Even if it means prolonging your divorce for another few years?"

Crystal relaxed and leaned back in her chair. "That won't happen."

Rick glanced at Patty and then looked back at Crystal. "Why is that?"

Crystal paused, and again her eyes traveled up and to the right. She looked back at Rick. "Because he'll tire of fighting and finally accept what I've offered him."

Patty asked the next question. "What is the address of your property in Arizona?"

Crystal looked surprised. "And why do you need to know that?"

"We need to check out all possibilities," said Patty. "The address?"

Crystal wrote it down and handed it to Patty. Rick stood up. Patty looked at Crystal.

"Does Grant have life insurance?"

"Of course he does. We both do. What does it matter?"

"We'll need the name and phone number of your agent."

Crystal quickly stood. "What exactly are you implying?"

"Not implying anything," said Patty. "Your husband seems to be missing. Asking questions may help us to understand why."

Crystal sat back down. "Well, I've given you all the information I have. You can talk with my attorney if you have more questions."

"Talk with your attorney?" asked Rick. "That seems an odd demand if something serious has happened to your husband. I should think you'd want to help."

Crystal fought for control of herself. "Oh, of course I do. I'm just tired, and this business with Grant is nerve-racking." She wrote something down and handed it to Patty. "That's our insurance agent."

"Thank you. We'll let you get on with your work."

Rick walked out and Patty turned to leave. "One last question. Do you know if Grant had any injuries that required metal implants?"

Crystal furrowed her brow in thought. "That's an odd question. I know he broke an ankle when he was younger and had a plate attached to his leg. That was before he met me."

Patty glanced at Rick before saying goodbye to Crystal. "Thanks again."

CHAPTER 10

Crystal picked up her phone and tapped in Blake's number on speed-dial. He answered. "Yeah?"

"The detectives were just here for the second time. Remind me how sure you are that you covered your tracks."

Blake exhaled loudly. "There's no way they can connect you or me to the murder. We used a lye solution that would have made a liquid mess of your ex within a few hours. There won't be prints on anything. So let it go. You are the wife, so expect them to want to talk with you."

"They asked if Grant had implants. Why would they want to know?"

"I don't know, Crystal. Just checking the boxes. You are making yourself sick over nothing."

"Yeah, I know you're right. I just hate being questioned."

"So live with it, Crystal."

"Yeah, okay. Before you go, Blake, I've got something else I need to talk with you about."

"What kind of something else? I've got things to do. I've got a couple of lawns to mow for my church followers."

"Kevin has a problem he wants fixed."

"Kevin? Why would I be interested in helping Kevin with his problems?"

"Because it's necessary. Remember that he knows about what we did. He's got information that could put us both away."

"As I recall," said Blake, "that was a few years ago when he played a small role in our plan, and he was paid for his service. Now he's what, Crystal? Threatening you? This is so indicative of some people nowadays. You pay them to take care of one small thing for you, and they want more money. They're never satisfied. Maybe Kevin needs the same treatment you've ordered for Grant."

"No, he doesn't. He'll keep his mouth shut if we help him out. He knows that if he says anything, he'll go to prison too. And what do you know about some people? Most of the people you know are addicts. Kevin works hard."

"I'm not interested in doing anything for Kevin, Crystal. We used him to get rid of Grant. Now tell him to go away."

"I can't, Blake. Kevin brings in a lot of money for me. He wants his wife, Bella, removed, and we're going to help him." Crystal was waiting for Blake's response when the line disconnected. She redialed and when her call went to voice mail, she left a message.

"This isn't a request, Blake. It has to be done. I've put Kevin off while we first concentrated on Grant. Now we need to help him. I have an idea on how Kevin can take care of Bella himself with very little input from you or me."

CHAPTER 11

Patty's cell phone rang. "It's the doc."

Rick sat back in his chair and listened to the conversation.

"Hi, Doc."

"Hey, Patty. You and Rick busy catching bad guys?"

"Hard to do, Doc, if we don't know who was murdered."

The doc laughed. "Let me help you out with that. According to Stryker, your victim is your missing man, Grant Wellingham."

"That's great, Doc," said Rick. "I'm sure the responsibles figured there was no way he'd ever be identified."

Patty laughed. "Heating the lye, filling the barrel, folding Grant into it, transporting the barrel to the dam and placing it in the water. All that effort, only to botch the job because they either didn't see the plate or didn't know that lye wouldn't dissolve it."

The doc spoke bluntly. "Like I've been saying, Mr. Grant Wellingham was one lucky man. Now the two of you need to bring justice to the people who did this to him."

"I can't say we'll be able to bring justice, but we will find and arrest those responsible. Thanks again, Doc."

"You're both welcome. Oh, about the notch in the sternum. There is no way that I can come up with one or two possible murder weapons. What I might be able to do is confirm whether something you find could have caused the notch and pierced the heart of our victim."

"That works for us, Doc. We'll let you know."

Rick quickly got his goodbye in too. "You've made my day, Doc. Thanks for helping us out with Mr. Lucky."

"Always happy to serve, Rick."

Patty ended the call. "I'll let the LT know we've got a name to go with our victim." She walked down the hall and found the lieutenant at his desk. A new plaque on the wall read "Special Olympics Southern Oregon Coach of the Year."

"Congratulations, LT, on your Coach of the Year recognition. Nice plaque."

The lieutenant broke into a large, relaxed smile, something Patty rarely saw. He turned and looked at the family photo and plaque. "Thanks, Detective. We had a great time." He turned back toward Patty and the smile vanished as he asked, "What's up? Got a break yet in the Barrel Bones case?"

"As a matter of fact, LT, we do. Stryker was able to identify the name of our victim. The bones belong to our missing Grant Wellingham."

"You have no DNA and yet have identified your victim by his Stryker device! That's a first for me, O'Toole. Makes for a very interesting case. Good work!"

"Thank you, sir, but to be fair, it was our victim who helped us out on this one."

"Have you and Rick discussed how best to use the Stryker information?"

"Not yet. Do you have a suggestion?"

"One. Think about keeping it quiet for a while. Let the wife know that the bones were identified as those of her missing husband. Observe how she reacts. Get a sense of whether she's genuinely distraught or is shocked that the bones were identified. She may lead you to other suspects who will also be shocked that you've identified their victim. There is a possibility that one will turn on the others."

"That's a great idea, LT. I'll take it back to Rick."

The lieutenant gave a nod. "You and Rick need to work fast. Experience tells me this may not be their first victim, nor their last. Be careful. You're looking for experienced killers."

"Always, LT. Oh, on another subject, Rick has a good friend he worked with visiting from Boston. His name is Chuck Spencer, and he'll be arriving here at the department about three. We'd like to take off early."

The lieutenant nodded. "Enjoy the visit."

Patty returned to her desk. Rick was on the phone with Chuck.

"Great, Chuck. Thanks for the update. We'll see you in a few hours." Rick looked up at Patty. "He just passed through Cave Junction and will meet with a real estate agent at one-thirty. He's still planning on being here about three."

"I'm looking forward to meeting him, Rick. I let the LT know we'd be leaving early. I also told him about the Stryker identification."

"I'll bet he was impressed," said Rick.

"He was, and said it was a first for him. He also said we should be careful. He gave me an idea for us to consider in how we move forward on the case."

"Great! What does he suggest?"

"We keep quiet about the Stryker plate for a while. Wait to get a reaction from Crystal. If she was involved in her husband's death, she'll be shocked to learn that we identified him. She may also panic."

Rick agreed. "And people who panic generally become sloppy. She may lead us to others who were involved. I like the LT's approach."

"I know we were looking forward to the weekend, Rick, but with this new information we need to put our plans on pause."

"I agree, Patty. Chuck will need a day to settle in, and then I'm sure he'd like to be brought in on the case."

"I'll call Crystal now and set something up for tomorrow. Given there's a chance she was not involved in his death, and the sensitivity of the message, I'll attempt to set up the appointment at her home."

Patty picked up her cell phone and tapped in Crystal's number. After four rings, the call went to voice mail. Hearing the tone, Patty left a message. "Mrs. Wellingham, we have new information about your husband. Please call so that we can schedule a time when Detective Starker and I might meet with you at your home."

Patty picked up a yellow pad and pen. "I'll start by letting her know that we've learned that Grant is deceased. I won't use the term 'murder' until we observe her response. If she's innocent, we may decide to go no further with questions until tomorrow."

"I agree. If she doesn't ask how, we'll have a fairly good indication that she knows something."

Patty looked up from her notes. "And if she does ask, I'll let her know he was murdered."

"If she's guilty," said Rick, "the conversation will be brief. She'll be eager to get rid of us and talk with her partners in crime."

Patty's cell phone lit up. "It's Crystal."

Rick sat back and listened to Patty's side of the conversation.

"Detective O'Toole. Hello, Crystal. Thank you for calling back. Detective Starker and I have new information about Grant. We want to meet with you as soon as possible. No. This is not information I wish to give you over the phone. Can we meet you at your home within the next hour? This is important. Okay. Twenty minutes at your office."

The call ended, and Patty filled Rick in on Crystal's side of the conversation. "She has an appointment in forty-five minutes and doesn't have time to go home first. So she wants to get us in and out quickly."

Rick stood up. "Her office is private, and there may be an agent there to comfort her if needed."

The detectives arrived at Crystal's office as expected. She greeted them in the lobby and asked the receptionist to hold her calls before leading the detectives back to her office. "Please sit down. Would either of you like coffee?"

They both declined the offer.

"Well," said Crystal, "I have an important client arriving in about twenty-five minutes. What information about Grant is so important you had to see me ASAP?"

Patty leaned forward and spoke softly. "We're sorry to have to tell you, Crystal, but we've found Grant, and he's deceased."

The detectives carefully observed Crystal as she sat upright in her seemingly frozen position. There was no initial reaction, facial or otherwise.

"Crystal?" asked Patty. "May I get you a drink of water?"

Crystal's eyes began to move rapidly about the room, as though she were looking for something.

"No," she said, and deeply inhaled. Then, with a tone of disbelief, she spoke. "So you found him?"

"We did," said Patty.

Crystal stumbled for the next thing to say. "Umm, are you certain it's him?"

"We are," said Patty.

"How?"

Patty glanced at Rick. "I'm not sure I know what you're asking, Crystal."

"Well, umm, how can you be sure that it's him?"

"The medical examiner's office has confirmed identification for us."

"Oh, I see."

"Is there someone we can call to be with you, Crystal?"

"Umm, no. I don't need anyone. I've got a client I need to prepare for. And then I've got to think about what to do next. I should call the insurance company and my attorney. Umm, you can leave. Thanks for letting me know."

Rick stood up. "Is there someone here at the office who can take care of your client for you? You've had quite a shock."

"No, no. I'll be okay. Thank you both for coming in."

Patty stood. "We'll need to ask you some questions, Crystal. I'll call tomorrow morning to set up a time tomorrow afternoon."

Crystal looked up at Patty and then stood. "Questions? What kind of questions?"

"Crystal, Grant Wellingham was murdered."

"Murdered? How do you know he was murdered?"

Rick provided the response. "We know by the manner of death."

Patty signaled to Rick that they should leave. "I'll call in the morning, and we'll set up a time to talk tomorrow afternoon. Are you sure we can't call someone to come stay with you?"

"I'm sure. I just need to be alone now and prepare for my client. Tonight, I'll think about what I need to do next."

On the drive back to their office, Patty commented first. "I am thinking about the fact that she hated him and working that into my thoughts about her reaction. She didn't ask where he was found, how he died, or how we identified him. And there was no immediate concern about her children learning that their father was murdered. What are your first thoughts?"

Rick glanced across the front seat at Patty and then put his eyes back on the road. "She's guilty. The only question is to what degree? She didn't ask how we identified him because she believed that identifying the body would not be possible. I think she was frantically trying to accept that what she thought was the perfect crime has unraveled a bit. Her thoughts now will be whether there's any way she can be linked to the murder."

Rick pulled into the parking lot, and Patty unhooked her seat belt. "Now all we have to do is find something that positively links her to the murder so that we can get a warrant to search her house, office, computers, and any place else that might hide evidence."

CHAPTER 12

At the agreed-upon time, Kevin's new client walked in and was greeted by the receptionist.

The large man spoke kindly. "I'm here to see Kevin."

Kevin heard his name and stepped out of the office. "Mr. Spencer?" he asked, extending his hand. "I'm Kevin. Please come in."

Chuck Spencer sat down across from Kevin. The receptionist came to the office door momentarily to offer Chuck coffee or tea.

"No, thanks." He sat with his hands folded in his lap.

Kevin picked up a pen. "Well, Mr. Spencer, or may I call you Chuck?"

"Sure."

"Great. You told me briefly when we initially spoke on the phone that you currently live in Boston. What brings you across the country to Brookings?"

"I have friends here."

Kevin made notes as he spoke. "So, are you considering a permanent move or would a place in Brookings be a second home?"

"I don't know yet."

"I see," said Kevin. "Who is your current employer?"

"I'm retired."

"Oh, that must be nice. Doing a lot of traveling?"

"A little."

"Okay," said Kevin as he continued to write. "Just a couple more questions and we can go view the condo. Do you own your home in Boston?"

"Yes."

"And if you decide to purchase in Brookings, will you be applying for a loan and putting twenty percent down?"

"Probably."

Kevin smiled. "You are a man of few words, Chuck. I like that." He stood up. "Let's go see the condo you called on. I have set up a couple other viewings after the condo so that you have a good idea as to what is available in our area."

Chuck followed Kevin to his car and climbed into the passenger seat.

Kevin pointed to a button above the seat handle. "I'm guessing you'd be a lot more comfortable putting the seat back. You must be, what, six-five or -six?"

Chuck put his seat back as he answered, "Yep."

Kevin took Chuck through the condo and then showed him two other properties. On their return to Kevin's office, his cell phone rang. "This is Kevin. Oh, hi. Police? What did they want? I can't talk about that now. I'll call you later." He glanced at Chuck. "Small problem at the office."

Chuck showed no reaction to the call. He followed the real estate agent back into the office, where Kevin sat down and picked up a pen.

"Have a seat," said Kevin.

"No, I need to take off."

Kevin put the pen down and stood up again. "Well, you seemed to like the condo better than the other properties. Do you agree?"

"Yes. Thanks for showing it to me. I need to think about this. I'll be in touch with my decision."

Kevin stepped around the side of his desk. "Well, don't you want to discuss terms so that you'll know the amount of your monthly mortgage payment and the amount down you'll need if you decide you'd like to make an offer?"

"No need. I'll let you know within the week if I want it."

Kevin followed Chuck to the front door. "Okay. That will be fine. I'll look forward to hearing from you." He walked back to his desk. He stood tall, then brought his arms up from his sides and over his head while taking a deep breath through his nose. He then slowly lowered his arms exhaling through his mouth. After two more times of deep breathing, he sat down and called Crystal. She answered.

"Kevin. You write up an offer?"

"Not yet. But I will. Your message said that the police spoke to you. What did they want?"

"They know, Kevin."

"Know what?"

"They know that Grant is not just missing. They know that he's dead."

"How? Blake said there was no way the cops could know who was in the barrel."

"I know, Kevin. But the cops know. So either they found fingerprints or someone told them. And that means either you or Blake."

Kevin yelled, "How can you possibly suspect me of ratting? I believed Blake when he told us there was no way to identify Grant or connect his murder to any of us. If anyone ratted, it must have been him. Have you talked to him?"

"I will, Kevin. Just stay calm. I'll talk to Blake and then call you back. Will you remain calm?"

"This is really, really bad, Crystal, and I don't like it at all."

"Kevin, will you just calm down? I'll talk to Blake. Wait for my call."

"Okay, but we've got to figure out how this happened." Kevin heard no response. "Crystal?"

She had disconnected and quickly called Blake. She knew he was talking with someone else when her call went directly to voice mail.

"Blake, it's Crystal. Call me as soon as you can. The police were here again. They know that Grant is dead."

Crystal fidgeted in her chair waiting for Blake to call. She opened a file and stared at it for thirty seconds before slamming it shut again. When her cell phone vibrated, she saw that Blake was calling her back.

"Blake. How can this happen?"

"What exactly did the cops say, Crystal?"

"They said that the medical examiner confirmed that Grant is dead and that he was murdered. How do they know, Blake? You assured me there'd be nothing left to identify."

"I don't know how they knew it was him, Crystal. I made up the lye and water mixture just like the instructions said to do. I even heated it over a hot fire out back. There shouldn't have been anything of him left."

"I'm not going down for murder because you messed up, Blake."

"Wait a minute, Crystal. None of us is going down for murder. Think about it. So they know it's Grant. Big deal. That's all they know. They didn't get fingerprints, or they'd have told you."

Crystal's response followed a brief hesitation. "Yeah, okay, I see what you're saying. So maybe I don't need to be so upset."

"That's right. It's just that now the cops are working on a homicide instead of a missing-person case. That's all, Crystal. No big deal."

Crystal nervously laughed. "You're right, Blake. I was so shocked that they figured out the body in the barrel was Grant's, I guess I couldn't think straight."

"So, we okay now, Crystal? No more panicky phone calls?"

"Yeah, Blake, I'm okay. I'll call Kevin back. He's pretty shook up."

"Listen, Crystal, you can't let Kevin panic. No telling what he'll do. He's a liability, you know."

"He won't be a problem, Blake. I'll calm him down. Thanks again." The phone disconnected.

* * *

"It's almost three o'clock," said Rick. "When Chuck gets here, I'd like to introduce him to the LT."

Patty nodded. "We'll have plenty to talk with Chuck about. He might be surprised to learn that we've had a gruesome murder here in quaint little Brookings. Think he'll be interested in hearing about it?"

"I'm sure he will. I'd like to know if he's ever uncovered a clue in the form of a Stryker device."

Patty's phone lit up. "It's Cindi Browning returning my call. Detective O'Toole."

"Hello, Detective. I hope you have good news."

"Good morning, Cindi. Detective Starker is here, so you're on speaker phone. I'm sorry, but the news we have is not good. We've found your brother."

Patty could hear no reaction. "Ms. Browning?"

"Yes, Detective, I'm here. Since I've not heard from Grant, I'm thinking that he just needed to get away and forgot to tell me."

"I'm very sorry to have you tell you that Grant is deceased."

"Oh, oh, my God. What happened to him? How?"

"Cindi, your brother was murdered."

Patty heard a loud gasp. "Murdered! How? By whom?"

"The cause of your brother's death is going to be very painful for you to hear. Is there a neighbor or friend who could sit with you while we're on the phone? You could ask someone and call me back when you're no longer alone."

"Yes, let me call my good friend. She'll come over and I'll call you back. Oh, dear, I just can't fathom someone wanting to hurt Grant."

"We're very sorry. Call me back when your friend is with you."

"Okay. I will."

As Patty ended the call, Rick stood up and walked toward the door. "Right on time, Chuck. You always were. How you doing, old buddy?"

Chuck smiled and held out his arms to embrace Rick. "A little wear and tear but nothing that can't be fixed with a few days on the coast." Chuck then looked at Patty. "This must be the partner I've heard so much about."

Patty rose. "Only the good, I hope." She extended her hand. "I'm Patty O'Toole. Rick's told me a lot about Boston's famous Chuck Spencer, and I'm looking forward to hearing lots of stories."

Chuck looked at Rick. "Well, I'll see what I can come up with. Maybe a few with this guy."

"Very few," laughed Rick. "Let's walk down the hall. I want to introduce you to our LT."

Patty began gathering her things to leave early with Rick and Chuck.

* * *

Rick, Patty, and Chuck stopped at Rick's place so that Chuck could unpack his belongings and settle in. While he was out of the room, Patty spoke with Rick about the Cindi Browning call. "She was clearly shocked."

"She was," said Rick. "It was a much different reaction from that of his wife."

"If she calls back after Chuck joins us, I'll step into the kitchen to talk with her. Cindi may have more to say about Crystal once she learns how her brother died."

"Okay. We should probably head out for dinner a little before five so that we beat the after-work rush."

Patty looked at her watch. "I'll keep track of the time."

"Thanks. I've got a dozen questions I want to ask Chuck as we catch up. It's sure great having him here."

"I can see that, Rick, and I'm very pleased that he's come. I'm interested in learning how his brief house-hunting went with the agent. I know he's like family to you and that his living out here, at least part-time, would be great for you both."

Rick smiled. "Yeah, that would be something special."

Patty's cell phone illuminated. "It's her." She accepted the call. "Detective O'Toole."

"Detective, this is Cindi. My good friend Anne is here with me, so I've got you on speaker phone."

"I'm glad that Anne can be with you."

"Please, Detective, tell me how Grant was killed."

"Your brother was killed with an instrument we've not yet identified. It pierced through his sternum and into his heart."

"Oh." Cindi's voice broke. "Where do I go to see him? I want to see him."

"I'm sorry, Cindi. Due to the condition of Grant's remains, you can't see him."

The tone of Cindi's voice changed as she continued. She became angry and loud. "Can't see him? I don't care what shape he's in. I want to see my brother."

Patty could hear Anne comforting her friend as Patty continued. "I'm sorry. What I'm about to tell you is going to be very difficult for you to hear. But I need you to hear it before you read about it in the newspaper. Grant's body was dismembered and then folded into a barrel of lye solution. The barrel was placed—"

Before Patty could go on, Cindi screamed. "No, no, no. Oh my God, no."

Anne took the phone. "Detective O'Toole, this is Anne. I need to hang up now."

"I understand, Anne. You may want to call Cindi's doctor and ask what you can give her to sleep. When she's calmer, please let her know that I'll call back tomorrow. There will be a few questions I'll need to ask."

"I'll do that, Detective. Thank you."

Chuck walked into the room and sat down across from Patty.

Rick got up. "What can I get you? Beer, wine, Irish whiskey?"

"I'll have a beer."

Rick then looked at Patty. "Chardonnay?"

"I'd like that," said Patty.

While Rick was getting the drinks, Chuck spoke to Patty. "Rick probably told you that I spent some time with a real estate agent earlier today. It gave me a chance to see some of Brookings. You sure live in a beautiful place."

"Thanks, Chuck. I've lived my whole life here and have never had reason to complain. The temperature stays between forty-five and sixty-five for a lot of the year. It often requires a vest or light jacket, but we don't have to shovel snow or deal with extreme heat and humidity. How did your time with the agent go? See anything you like?"

"I did. There's a condo on the ocean that I'm interested in. The price is steeper than I'd like, but I may find out if the owner's willing to come down in exchange for a short escrow period."

Rick walked in and handed a glass of Chardonnay to Patty and a porter to Chuck.

Chuck looked at the label. "Black Butte Porter. You remembered."

Rick smiled. "I remember a lot."

Patty sipped her wine and set the glass down. "Chuck was just talking with me about the properties he saw earlier today, including a condo on the ocean."

Rick looked at Chuck. "Like what you saw?"

"I liked all three. If I decide on getting something here, I'll probably make an offer on the condo. I like the peacefulness of this town. You must have very little crime."

Chuck watched Patty and Rick look at each other. "Tell me you don't have regular shootings."

Rick moved his head. "No, nothing like that. However, Patty and I are working on a homicide that includes an interesting victim ID. We'll bring you in on it while you're here if you're interested."

"Sure I am. Tell me what you've got."

Rick proceeded to tell Chuck about the missing Grant Wellingham and finding the bones in the barrel of lye. "Then, for the most interesting part: The lye solution made finding DNA impossible. Yet we were still able to identify him. He had a Stryker plate screwed to his fibula."

Chuck nodded his head and smiled. "And Stryker has an identification number on each of their plates and implants."

"Yes, how did you know?"

"We had a couple of cases in which the deceased had a Stryker piece screwed onto the body. In both of our cases, however, we'd already identified the deceased. Your case is unique in that it is the only manner in which you've identified the victim. Several years ago, I took a course about the use of identifying hardware."

Rick slowly shook his head. "I guess I missed that class because it was the ME who told us. Without that piece of stainless steel, we'd have had no way to identify our victim."

"That," Patty said, "is information we are not at this time releasing to the public. We can talk more about the case over dinner. Still interested?"

"Absolutely," said Chuck.

Rick smiled. "Chuck, do you remember the joke we played on the captain suggesting that we were using a psychic to solve our cases?"

"I do." Chuck looked at Patty. "That was one of the better jokes we played. Hard to believe more than twenty years have passed since then. What caused you to think of it now?"

"Well," said Rick, "I'm about to play a similar joke on our chief. We have a local psychic. I stopped in a few days ago to pick up some brochures, and I still have the crystal ball you and I used in Boston."

"Have you been waiting on me before playing this out?"

"No, but since you're here, you might enjoy the chief's reaction as much as we do. A few weeks ago, he asked Patty how she and I solve so many cases. I plan on placing the crystal ball and a few brochures on my desk. I'll also put a couple brochures in the break room."

Patty listened intently while the two guys enjoyed recreating the joke. "I hope that we're all in the room when the chief looks at the top of Rick's desk."

Chuck laughed. "Yeah, I have to admit I'm enjoying just thinking about it. We were doing things like that all the time in Boston. Mostly to each other. I like to think it saved the sanity of at least a few cops."

"I like it," said Patty. "I hope the chief will too. It will say a lot about his disposition." She looked at her watch. "Time to head over to Dewy's for dinner."

Chuck looked at Rick. "Dewy's?"

Rick spelled the name of the bar for Chuck and smiled. "It's a downtown bar and restaurant with great food. Popular with law enforcement."

"I'll bet."

The restaurant was within a few blocks of the police station. A waitress quickly seated them at a table and provided menus. She asked about drinks and Rick ordered. "Chardonnay, porter beer, and a Coke."

"So tell me more about your case," said Chuck.

Rick looked at Patty. "Why don't you start?"

"Okay. The initial call was about a barrel that was found in a dammed reservoir not far from here. The contents turned out to be human bones in a lye solution. We discovered, by means of the Stryker hardware, that the victim is a local contractor, Grant Wellingham. He was in the process of divorce with a local real estate broker who has a posh downtown office housing several agents. Initially, she told us that her divorce was going smoothly. We learned from the vic's sister, attorney, and employer that the divorce was anything but smooth."

"So," said Chuck, "she was lying from your first meeting."

Rick nodded. "The vic had been reported missing by his sister before we found the bones. The soon-to-be ex became upset when we told her we found her husband, but her concern did not seem to be for the reason one would think. She couldn't understand how we were sure that the body we found was her husband's. She's definitely hiding something."

The waitress set down the drinks, and Chuck took a drink of his beer. "And you're keeping the Stryker information from her?"

"We're keeping that information from everyone," said Patty. "We believe she has something to do with the death and that she did not carry it out alone. We're hoping she'll soon contact her accomplices."

"Good tactic," said Chuck. "Pit them against each other."

"That's the idea," said Rick. "We don't have much else right now, so we hope it works."

The waitress stepped up to their table. "Ready to order?"

"We are," said Rick. He indicated to Patty that she go first.

"I'll have the fish and chips."

Rick nodded at Chuck. "I'll have the steak with a baked potato and dinner salad."

The waitress turned toward Rick. "And you?"

Rick pointed toward the menu. "I'll have this surf and turf with fries. I'd also like water for each of us."

"Will do," she said while collecting the menus.

"What's your next step?" asked Chuck.

Patty set down her wine glass. "That's the problem. We've got nothing solid on the wife, and we need to seize her phone and computer to find who's in this with her." Before she could go on, Chuck's cell phone vibrated.

"This is the real estate agent. Mind if I take it?"

"Not at all," said Patty. The caller was loud enough that Patty could hear the whole conversation.

"Hello, Kevin."

"Hello, Chuck. Do you have a minute?"

"Sure, as long as it's quick. I'm having dinner with friends."

"I won't be long. Another condo has come on the market. It's in the same building but in a superior location. It's a first-floor end unit. The price is the same, but I think it will go quickly because of the location and upgrades. I can get you in this evening or tomorrow morning if you're interested."

"Let's make it early tomorrow morning,"

The agent paused. "Can you make it at eight or eight-thirty?"

"Eight works. I'll meet you at your office."

Chuck ended the call. "Seems another condo has just come on the market. I might move on it since it's first-floor."

Rick smiled. "You just don't want to schlepp groceries up two or three flights."

Chuck affirmed Rick's suggestion. "Got that right. I'm not as agile as I used to be. One of the reasons to retire."

CHAPTER 13

Crystal sat back in her chair and called Kevin. "Hi, Kevin. I'm calling you back as I said I would."

Kevin sighed and blurted out a response. "That was this morning."

"I know, Kevin, but Blake can be difficult to reach."

"Okay, okay, what did he say?"

"Well, he was very sensible, as always. He reminded me that it doesn't matter that the police know the bones were Grant's. What matters is that they don't know who killed him. Actually, confirming the deceased is Grant makes life a lot easier for me. I can collect the life insurance and get on with my life. We can all get on with our lives." Kevin was silent. "Kevin, you there?"

"Yeah, yeah. I'm here."

"You okay then?"

"Yeah. I'm okay, I guess. So this means we can move forward with solving my problem."

"Well, Kevin, I don't know about that. Maybe we should wait until Grant's murder is old news."

"No, Crystal. Blake is right. We have nothing to worry about. You said you had an idea for me. What is it?"

"I don't like talking about it over the phone. Will you be in the office tomorrow?"

"Yeah. I've got a showing at eight. Why don't I come in at seven-thirty?"

"That's early, Kevin, but I will make it. I'll see you at seven-thirty."

The following morning, Chuck walked into the lobby just before eight to meet with Kevin. The receptionist wasn't in yet. He sat down to wait and could hear voices. One was that of a woman. The other was a man's. The sounds he heard expressed agitation and were raised enough periodically that Chuck recognized one voice as Kevin's.

Kevin sounded demanding. "I want her gone, Crystal. Quid pro quo. Remember?"

The front door opened as the secretary walked in. "Good morning. May I help you?"

Hearing the secretary's greeting, Kevin stepped out of Crystal's office and saw Chuck. "Oh, Mr. Spencer. I didn't know you'd come in. I'll be right there."

Chuck smiled. "No problem."

Kevin stepped back into Crystal's office. "I'll plan something using your idea. It could work."

Crystal smiled. "Let me know if she goes for it."

Kevin walked down the hall to greet Chuck. "How are you today?"

"Good."

"Shall we take my car? I'm right out front."

"No, I know where we're going. I'll meet you there."

The condo was a five-minute drive. Chuck walked through the front door noting the differences from the first condo they viewed. Kevin entered and began pointing out some specific features.

"These hardwood floors are beautiful, and the marble windowsills are a classy touch. Because this is a corner unit, you'd have a dynamite view up the coast."

Chuck withheld comment and looked at the bedrooms. Once satisfied, he and Kevin left the unit.

Kevin stopped to lock the front door. "Do you have any questions?"

"No."

"Well, okay. Which condo do you like best?"

Chuck turned around and nodded toward the front door. "This one."

Kevin smiled. "Should I keep looking for you?"

"No."

Kevin's smile fell flat. "I don't understand. Have you changed your mind about buying?"

"No. I'll take this one."

"Oh," said Kevin. "That's great! Do you have time now to go back to the office and sign the paperwork?"

"Yep."

Chuck met Kevin at his office, sat down, and sent a quick text to Rick. *Writing an offer. Will stop by when I'm done.*

Kevin brought the purchase agreement form up on his computer. "Okay. Let's discuss terms."

Before Kevin could go on, Chuck interrupted. "I'll offer twenty thousand less than they're asking and pay customary closing costs. I'll put forty percent down and close in two weeks. The sale will be contingent upon my approval of a home inspection report and the last twelve months of HOA minutes."

Kevin jotted down Chuck's requirements. "You've done this before," he said.

"Yep."

Kevin began filling in the online contract. As he proceeded, Crystal stuck her head in and waited for him to look up before she said anything. "Spoke with Blake. Mushrooms will work."

Chuck sat quietly, looking straight ahead while Crystal spoke. Kevin acknowledged Crystal's statement and continued putting information into the computer. A while later, Chuck signed the offer and associated documents and drove to the P.D.

Rick looked up when Chuck walked in. "You made an offer."

"I did."

"That's great. How much time does the seller have to respond?"

"I'm giving them forty-eight hours. If this goes through, I'll have a place just a few blocks from here and on the ocean."

Rick grinned. "Just like old times. And with an ocean view, Patty and I will be over often."

"If this goes through, buddy, you and Patty can come over any time. I'll probably spend half the year here. For now, let's talk about your case."

* * *

Kevin had a smile on his face as he drove home. He'd written an offer that he was sure would result in a much-needed commission. He'd also satisfied himself after talking with Crystal that he was safe from any discovery linking him to Grant's death. Now for plan B. As usual, he found no one else at home. Kevin took a beer out of the refrigerator, sat down in front of the TV and waited for Bella to arrive home.

CHAPTER 14

The following morning, Rick arrived early at the office and placed a few of the psychic brochures in the break room. He placed a couple others on his desk next to a crystal ball. When Patty and Chuck arrived, Chuck immediately recognized the crystal sphere.

"That brings back fond memories. Maybe it will help you and Patty with your Barrel Bones case."

Patty put her hands around the glass piece and pretended to gaze into it. "How is this supposed to work? If it will help with our case, I'll tell it whatever is necessary."

Before Patty could go on, the lieutenant walked into the room with a brochure.

"I stopped in the break room for coffee and found this." His eyes moved to the top of Rick's desk. "Guess I don't need to ask where it came from. Are you moonlighting, Rick?"

Patty removed her hands from the desktop icon.

Rick smiled. "No, LT. No time for that." He let the lieutenant in on the fun with an abbreviated version of their plan.

There was silence in the room as the lieutenant thought about what he'd just been told. He turned to walk out of the office, paused, and looked back. "I'll give the chief reason to stop in sometime this morning."

"Thank you, LT," said Patty.

Rick smiled. "That would be great."

About forty minutes later, the chief walked in.

"Chief? Good morning," said Patty.

"Good morning." He looked at Chuck. Rick stood up.

"Chief, this is Chuck Spencer, a good friend of mine. We worked together at Boston PD."

Chuck extended his hand. "Good to meet you, sir."

The chief shook Chuck's hand. "Good to meet you, Chuck. What brings you to Brookings?"

"I've just retired, and I'm catching up with good friends as I decide what to do next."

"How do you like it here on the edge of the world?"

"It's beautiful, Chief. I like it enough to want to spend a lot more time here. Yesterday I submitted an offer on a condo."

"Well, I hope that works out for you. We can always use more retired law enforcement in Curry County. Since you worked with Rick, I'm sure you'll understand why we're lucky to have him and Patty. They have quite a reputation for solving their cases."

The chief turned to continue the conversation with Rick and Patty. He stopped short and became silent as he stared at the psychic paraphernalia. Everyone was quiet as the chief walked to Rick's desk and picked up one of the pamphlets. He looked at the crystal ball and then toward Rick.

"Care to enlighten me as to what all this is about?"

"Yes, Chief. Patty mentioned to me that you inquired as to how it is we solve all of our cases." Rick said no more, and there was silence in the room as the chief ruminated on Rick's words.

After what seemed like several minutes to Patty, a small grin showed up on the chief's face. "Just make sure to include in your case reports any and all information you glean from this source."

There was a sense of relief in the air, and Rick and Patty laughed. "Yes, Chief. We'll do that."

Silence briefly filled the room following the chief's exit. Then Rick, Patty, and Chuck all smiled.

"Well," said Rick, "I like him."

Patty agreed. "I think we are going to enjoy working for our new chief."

* * *

Bella arrived home about nine, three hours later than the end of her work day. Kevin was waiting. He greeted her in the living room with a glass of Chardonnay.

"Hi, hon. How was your day?"

Bella accepted the glass and sat down. "Like any other day. Nothing special. And yours?"

"Pretty good. I wrote an offer. But I don't want to talk about work. I'd like to talk about something we can do together that you like to do."

Bella looked up. "Really? What is that?"

"Let's go mushroom-picking. It's the season, and I know how much you enjoy it."

Bella set her glass down on the coffee table. "It's funny you brought that up. I was just talking about mushroom-picking to someone I know from the office. He doesn't like mushrooms and therefore wasn't very interested. But, as you know, I enjoy the time in the forest picking them as much as the act of preparing and cooking mushroom soup."

Kevin smiled. "So, you up for the two of us going on a mushroom hike?"

"Yeah," said Bella. "I wouldn't want to go alone, so the two of us going together will be fine."

Kevin drank the rest of his beer. "How about this Saturday?"

Bella brought her hands up in front of her and studied her baby pink acrylic fingernails. "Sure. I can go on Saturday. Just don't get any ideas that this is some kind of a date."

Kevin smiled. "I won't think of it as a date at all, Bella. It will be a time for reflection on what I need to do to move forward."

* * *

Kevin called Crystal the following day. She was in her office and took Kevin's call.

"Good morning, Kevin."

"Hey, Crystal. I think your idea is going to work. Bella has agreed to go mushroom-picking with me on Saturday."

"That's good, Kevin. Have you thought about exactly what you're going to do? How will you get her to eat the wrong mushrooms?"

"I've given it a lot of thought. Bella and I have been mushroom-picking many times. We've seen the good mushrooms and identified those that are poisonous. She'll be picking lots of good mushrooms. I will too, but I'll also pick a few known poisonous ones. When we get home, she'll make a soup and, when she's out of the room, I'll put the poisonous mushrooms in the pot."

"That sounds like a great idea, Kevin. But how do you keep from poisoning yourself?"

"Oh, well, I don't like mushrooms. I've never eaten Bella's mushroom soup. She won't think anything about it, and I'll eat something else for dinner."

"Okay," said Crystal. "That sounds like a good plan. I'll let Blake know to call you and arrange to carry Bella out of your place and into his car at the right time. You'll go with Blake to the place he chooses to bury the body. That okay with you?"

"Yeah. That works."

"Good," said Crystal. "Stick with the plan and call me if anything goes wrong."

"Will do, Crystal. I feel like a huge weight has been lifted from my shoulders."

Kevin heard the line disconnect. He got ready for the day and drove to his office.

* * *

Chuck walked into the detectives' office at about nine.

"Looks like I'm going to own a place here."

Patty glanced at Rick and Chuck. "Your offer was accepted!"

"They countered five thousand higher, and I accepted."

Rick stood and shook Chuck's hand. "Congratulations."

Chuck nodded. "Thanks. There are a number of calls I now need to make, so I'll go back to your place, if that works for you."

"No problem," said Rick as he looked up at Patty.

She responded, "We've got an empty office here if you want to use it. It's just a desk and a chair. No landline."

"That would be great." Chuck held up his cell phone. "No need for a landline. I use this exclusively."

"The office is just down the hall," said Rick. "I'll show you."

While Rick was gone, Patty called the number for the real estate office handling Crystal and Grant's second home in Arizona. The call was answered on the first ring.

"Sunset Real Estate and Property Management. How can I help you?"

"I'd like to speak with Sandy Simons."

"I'll check whether Sandy is in. May I tell her who's calling?"

"This is Detective Patty O'Toole with the Brookings, Oregon police department."

"Oh! Please hold, Detective. I'll transfer your call to Sandy's phone."

After a brief wait, the agent picked up. "Sandy Simons."

Patty introduced herself. "I'm calling about a property you manage for Grant and Crystal Wellingham."

"The Wellinghams are my clients. How can I help you?"

"Is the property occupied at this time?"

"Please don't take this the wrong way, Detective, but I'll need proof that you are who you say you are before I can answer your questions."

"I understand, Ms. Simons. Does my phone number show up on your phone?"

"Yes. It does."

"Okay. I'll give you the number for the Brookings Police Department. You can call and confirm who I am, then call me back at this number."

"Yes. Okay, I'll call now."

Within a few minutes, Patty's cell phone rang.

"Thank you for your understanding, Detective."

"No problem. Now, is the Wellinghams' property occupied?"

Patty heard clicking from the computer keyboard. "No, it's vacant. And hasn't been rented for at least five years. We periodically receive a call to clean and prepare the house for the Wellinghams when they come during the winter."

"When is the last time anyone was in the house?"

"It was three months ago."

"Thank you, Ms. Simons. That's all I need."

"Detective, before you go, can you tell me why you are calling about the house?"

"I can tell you that Mr. Wellingham has died. We are doing a routine investigation for any clue as to what may have caused his death. Thank you again for your help."

"You're welcome, Detective."

Rick and Chuck walked into the office as Patty ended the call. She sipped her coffee before asking Chuck about his introduction. "So, did the chief try to recruit you?"

Chuck nodded. "He mentioned it, but I assured him that I have no itch to get back into the game, at least not as an employee. I'll freely share my experience with you two and let it go at that."

Patty glanced toward Rick. "And we appreciate any sharing of your experience you can give. I called the property management company for the Wellinghams' Arizona property. Their house is empty. I'm going to ask the LT if we can enlist the help of Tucson PD to check the place out for us."

"Good idea," said Rick. "While you do that, I'll call the insurance company and find out how much Crystal will receive."

The lieutenant was on his phone. Patty stood outside the office until he completed the call.

"Come in, O'Toole. How's the case going?"

"We're working on it. The Wellinghams own a second home in Tucson, AZ. The property manager says that it sits vacant during the summer months when the Wellinghams are not there. I'd like for someone to take a look inside. What do you think of my calling Tucson PD and asking them to send someone to the house?"

"I think that's a good idea, Detective. Call their detective and tell him about the lye solution and the unknown weapon. He or she will know what to look for."

"Thanks, LT. I've let Chuck Spencer use the vacant office we have. His offer on the condo was accepted, and he needs to make some calls. Rick and I have told Chuck about the Barrel Bones case. I'm hoping he'll come up with something that may help us find the responsible."

"So Chuck is interested in helping out. That's good."

When Patty returned to the office, Rick and Chuck were discussing what to do for dinner.

"If you'll barbeque them," offered Chuck, "I'll pick up a few steaks on my way to your place."

Rick glanced at Patty.

She nodded. "I can smell them already. Regarding work, I spoke with the LT. He thinks it's a good idea to have Tucson PD check on the Wellinghams' house."

"Tucson PD?" asked Chuck.

Rick explained while Patty made the call. After her call, Rick commented on the life insurance.

"She's insured for five hundred thousand. He was too until three months ago when his insurance was increased."

"Increased to what?" asked Patty.

"It was doubled."

Patty opened the file to write. "That's enough for motive. Did you tell them that the death was being investigated?"

"I did. They won't pay out on the policy until first checking with us. And they won't pay to a beneficiary convicted of murdering the insured."

"That," said Patty, "is something I doubt many beneficiaries know."

Chuck stood up. "You can bet that Crystal Wellingham doesn't. I've got a few more calls to make. Let me know when you're ready to call it a day."

CHAPTER 15

Kevin was sitting at a kitchen table. "Ready to go, Bella?"

"In a minute, Kevin. Don't rush me. I'm looking for my foraging bag."

"I'm not trying to rush you. Take as much time as you need, dear."

"And don't 'dear' me. This is not a date. I'm looking forward to a relaxing walk through the forest and collecting delectable items for my dinner." Bella walked into the kitchen. "I found my bag, but my pocketknife isn't in it. Do you have one I can use?"

"Sure, I'll get the one from my bedside table." Kevin retrieved the knife and took it to Bella. "You can use this. Do you have a toothbrush in your bag?"

"No, I guess I need one of those too."

Kevin opened his backpack. "I've got two. Here's one you can use. I've also got snacks and water for us."

Bella laughed. "Everything but the kitchen sink. Okay, let's go before you suggest something else I've forgotten."

A couple hours later, Bella and Kevin were busy picking mushrooms. As the afternoon wore on, Kevin called out to Bella, "My bag's about two-thirds full. How about yours?"

Hearing no response, Kevin walked to where Bella was carefully digging up a mushroom. "You about ready to call it a day?"

"Don't rush me, Kevin. We'll go when I'm ready."

"No problem, Bella. I'll keep picking if you want to stay longer."

Bella carefully used her toothbrush to clear dirt off the mushroom before bagging it. "Oh, alright. Let's go home. Being out here with you is like being with a little kid."

Kevin couldn't remain silent any longer. "How would you know what it's like to be with a child?"

Bella's face turned a slight shade of red as she narrowed her eyes at him. "Just take me home, Kevin. I've had enough of you for one day. And when we get home, stay out of the kitchen. I plan to put on a little music and make myself a delicious pot of soup."

"No problem, Bella. I'll be sure to stay out of your way. I made myself a sandwich this morning and left it in the refrigerator."

The ride home was quiet. Upon arrival, Bella took both bags of mushrooms and hurried into the kitchen. Kevin grabbed a beer from the refrigerator. He retired to his chair on the deck and waited.

Two hours had passed when a text popped up on Kevin's phone. It was from Bella. *I've got to run to the store for an ingredient. Don't mess up my kitchen making your sandwich. My soup is finished, and I've left it warming on the stove.*

Kevin smiled and texted back. *I won't. As I previously stated, I made a sandwich this morning. I'll just take it out of the refrigerator when I'm hungry. I won't touch anything of yours.* Hearing the front door open and close, Kevin hurried downstairs to the kitchen. He chopped the deadly mushrooms he'd picked into small pieces and dropped them into the cooking soup. He grabbed another beer and returned to his deck chair.

* * *

The steaks sizzled on Rick's grill. Patty put a bowl of potato salad on the table, and Chuck placed a loaf of garlic bread in the oven.

Rick called out, "Steaks are ready."

Patty brought him a platter. "I'll hold this while you put the steaks on it. The table's set, and Chuck's garlic bread will be ready in a couple of minutes. They look fabulous, Rick."

"They smell good too. Hope I've cooked them right for everyone."

Patty looked down at the steaks. "We all mentioned medium-rare, and it looks like that's what you've prepared. They'll be great."

When they were all sitting around the table, Patty wanted to hear more from Chuck. "Rick knows a lot about you, Chuck, but I don't. Care to talk about your career?"

Chuck swallowed. "Well, if you really want to know, I'll start at the beginning. I joined the Marine Corps immediately after graduating high school. Four years later, I was a sergeant and not ready to make the Corps a career. So I applied for a position with Boston PD. I was soon promoted to sergeant and found myself comfortable with law enforcement as a career choice. I was catching bad guys and making a difference. Ten years later, I was honored with a promotion to the prestigious SWAT team. That's when my life completely changed, and I began living every day on the edge. On the SWAT team, we were facing gang activity almost on a daily basis. It was a constant adrenaline rush. As you know, when a member of the public is presented with a fight-or-flight situation, the tendency is to run. In our law enforcement positions, when we're faced with the same situation, we move toward the fight. As a SWAT officer, I never slept through the night without a call. Last year, after thirty years with the PD and fifteen with SWAT, I was ready to find out what life is like without the stress of non-stop homicides." Chuck looked at Patty. "Now here I am, ready to spend time relaxing on the southern Oregon coast."

Patty sat a bit stunned. "I don't know what to say. Your description of work is something I've never come close to experiencing here. That isn't to say we haven't had a few murders, nor that I've not looked into the eyes of pure evil, but those incidents were the exceptions to the rule."

Rick put down his fork. "I can attest to the fact, Chuck, that life here will be a whole different world than what you're used to. I just hope you don't get bored."

Chuck laughed. "Bored? I don't think so. But tell you what, you and Patty bring me into a case now and then, and I promise not to complain about any lack of action."

Rick looked at Patty and raised his eyebrows. "I think we can accommodate that suggestion. Can I get either of you another beer?" Chuck nodded and handed Rick his empty bottle.

Patty lifted her bottle. "I'm still working on this one."

When Rick returned with the drinks, Chuck took a swallow of his and set the bottle down. "I've got a question on your Barrel Bones case. You've mentioned speaking with the wife of the deceased, Crystal, and mentioned she's in real estate. What firm does she work for?"

"CLW," said Patty. "Crystal is the owner-broker. Is she the agent you're working with?"

"No, but I am working with an agent in her office."

"Who's that?" asked Rick.

"Kevin Lacky. I've met him at his office a couple of times. I arrived early, before the receptionist, on the day I signed my offer. I could hear a bit of conversation in one of the offices and recognized Kevin's voice. The other voice was that of a woman. At one point, Kevin raised his voice and said what sounded to me like 'I want her gone.' I then heard a bit more of the conversation including him saying, 'quid pro.' He dropped his voice after that, but I'm assuming the word I didn't hear was 'quo.' Quid pro quo."

Rick sat back in his chair. "'I want her gone' and 'quid pro quo.' He could be talking about a real estate deal. Do you know if the woman he was talking to was Crystal?"

Chuck closed his eyes momentarily, opened them, and said, "Yes, I'm sure he referred to her once as Crystal."

"The victim," Patty said, "is male. So the conversation doesn't seem to pertain to the death of Grant. But they are curious phrases."

"Just something I figured you should know," said Chuck. "I found the conversation to be a bit odd."

Rick nodded. "I do too. If Crystal and Kevin are connected to Grant's murder, there may be another homicide in the works."

"We'll add that information to our file," said Patty. "Maybe you can find a reason to meet Kevin again at his office, Chuck, and ask him about what you heard."

"I thought the very same thing. I'll do that."

When dinner was finished, Patty stood to clear the dishes. "Returning to the subject of dinner, does anyone want dessert?"

Rick patted his belly. "I'm pretty stuffed."

"Yeah," said Chuck. "Everything was great!"

"It's apple pie."

"Well, when you put it like that," said Chuck, "I'll have a piece."

"Count me in, too, Patty."

Patty turned to walk into the kitchen but momentarily turned back toward the guys. "With a scoop of vanilla ice cream on top?"

Rick looked at Chuck. "Is there any other way to eat apple pie?"

During the dessert, Patty asked Chuck about his knives. "Rick told me how you have sat in a room related to a crime and manipulated your balisong to help you think. I'm interested in knowing more."

Chuck reached around the back of his jeans and pulled out a balisong. He began flipping it open and closed. The action caused a sound similar to a click-click. "It helps me think."

"Why?" asked Patty.

"It might be the clicking noise, repetitive action, familiar feel of the knife, or all three. It helps clear my head of everything else so that I can concentrate on the work at hand. When I'm sitting in a room looking for clues to a crime, it's necessary that I fully concentrate, forgetting about everything else going on in my life at that moment."

"That's very interesting, and I think I understand. One of the reasons I enjoy Pilates or yoga is that in addition to providing exercise, they require me to focus. They give my mind some respite from anything I might be worried or concerned about. And at times, I do come up with an idea I'd not previously thought of about a case."

"That's it," said Chuck. "It clears the mind to allow intense focus on one thought."

"When I watch you flipping the balisong, it looks dangerous. Does it require a lot of practice?"

Chuck manipulated the knife again. "It is dangerous, and it does require practice. There are knives with dull points made specifically for practicing."

Rick listened to the exchange between Chuck and Patty. "Tell Patty about your other knives, Chuck."

"Well, I am somewhat of a collector, I have a craw bit knife that also makes a clicking noise when opened and closed, but I think Rick's probably referring to my small collection of Half Face Blades. The knives are as famous for the materials used to make the handles as they are for the blades. The one I most recently purchased is an Enforcer. Two materials used to make the grip are dyed giraffe bone and birdseye maple. I'll bring the knives with me on a trip out here if you're interested in my talking more about them."

"I am interested. They sound beautiful, like works of art."

"That they are," said Chuck. "Now, enough about me. I already know a lot about Rick's life, and he's told me a little about you. I knew you'd have green eyes and brown hair, but I'd like to hear your story."

Patty looked at Rick and then back to Chuck. "Well, okay. I grew up here in Brookings. My father died when I was young. After graduating high school, I went on to college. I cannot remember a time when I ever thought of doing anything other than law enforcement. So I got my degree in criminal justice, applied to Brookings PD, was hired, and I've worked here since."

"According to Rick, you're a great detective."

Patty looked over at Rick and smiled before Chuck continued on. "He's also told me that you have a daughter."

"I do. Her name is Rebecca. We call her Becky or Bec. She's a part-time teacher and attends college classes toward another degree. Sometimes I think she's waiting for an epiphany to enlighten her on what it really is she wants to do with her life. Her father left us when Becky was about eight. I then changed my surname back to my maiden name, O'Toole, and out of concern for Becky, gave her the O'Toole name. I was very lucky to have my mom nearby, allowing me to go to work while she took care of Becky. My mom, Maggie, is now in her mid-seventies and lives here in Brookings. I know she'd like to meet you, so we'll have you both over for dinner one day soon. Well, that's my life's Reader's Digest version, and it's not much different from the longer version."

Chuck nodded toward Rick. "How do you like working with this guy?"

Patty laughed. "I have enjoyed working with Rick since the day he arrived here from Boston. He brings a wealth of experience far greater than mine. He and I each have unique ways in which to mindfully investigate crimes, and together we've been very successful."

Chuck smiled. "Successful to the point of making the chief wonder about your secret solve methods."

"Yeah," said Patty. "I guess so."

"You mentioned earlier about one case you've not been able to solve. What was that?"

"Rick can tell this one."

"About a year ago, we found a human hand that had been buried in the sand and dirt along one of our beaches. Between high tides and the sand, we were not able to identify the victim. So it remains our one unsolved case."

* * *

Kevin called Crystal to update her on Bella's condition.

"So we went mushroom-hunting as planned. Bella was in the process of making her soup when she realized she lacked one ingredient and had to go to the store. While she was gone, I dropped the deadly mushrooms into the soup pot. When Bella returned home, she finished cooking her soup, sat down at the table with a glass of Chardonnay, and ate a full bowl of her concoction. She's been pretty sick for the past two hours, and she's asking me to take her to the hospital."

"Kevin, think carefully. Are you sure that what she ate will kill her? She may just throw it all up and be fine."

"No, Crystal. She's not going to be fine. I'm sure that what I put into her soup will do the job. She's fading in and out of consciousness. So I'm thinking it's okay if I leave. She's moaning a lot, and I really don't want to hear it. I'll go to the office for a while and call the ambulance when I return home."

"That sounds like our plan is working, provided you're sure she won't recover. Why don't I ask Blake to stop by before you call the ambulance?"

"If you think it's necessary."

"I do, Kevin. You must be back home in two hours to let Blake in. You got that?"

"Okay. I will."

Blake showed up at Kevin's condo at the scheduled time. He walked upstairs and looked at Bella lying on the bathroom floor. He held his finger to her carotid artery.

"Should I call the ambulance now, Blake?"

"No. I'm leaving. I want you to wait fifteen minutes and then make the call."

"Leaving? But Crystal said that the plan was for us to put her in your car. We were going to bury her someplace."

Blake put his hands on his head. "Are you nuts? She's a mess. I'd never get rid of the evidence in my car. An ambulance will take her to the funeral home. Just tell them she wanted to be cremated."

"Okay," said Kevin. "Do you think she'll remain unconscious?"

Blake looked at Kevin. "No."

"Oh, that's not good. Maybe I should wait longer before calling 911."

"Just do like I told you, Kevin. She's not unconscious. She's dead."

Blake left, and Kevin walked back downstairs to the kitchen. He took a beer and his sandwich from the refrigerator, popped the top on the beer, and sat down at the kitchen table. Fifteen minutes later Kevin tapped 911 into his phone.

After the first responders had left and Bella's body had been taken away, Kevin called Crystal. She seemed eager to hear from him.

"Everything go as planned, Kevin?"

"More or less. But it wasn't pretty."

"Well, Kevin, what did you expect?"

"I don't know, I guess I didn't expect the mess. It will take me days to put the bathroom back in order."

"Well, it's done. Are you coming into work tomorrow?" Crystal waited for Kevin's response. "Kevin? Are you still there?"

"Yeah. But listen, there could be a problem."

Crystal's voice changed to one of concern. "Problem? What problem?"

Kevin spoke hesitantly, not sure of what to say. "The deputy medical examiner was here to pronounce Bella dead. He said there would probably be an autopsy. We didn't plan on there being an autopsy, Crystal."

"Well, Kevin, I don't think we have too much to worry about. The medical examiner will learn that Bella ate poisonous mushrooms. Lots of people have mistakenly died that way. We discussed this and how you should respond if asked about it. Do you remember?"

"Yeah, Crystal, I know. I will talk about how much Bella loved picking and cooking mushrooms. And how much she enjoyed the soup, and I didn't. But she was pretty sick, and I waited hours before calling 911. I'm worried, Bella. I don't want to go to prison."

"Calm down, Kevin. I'll talk with Blake. I'm sure he'll have a logical response. I'll try getting hold of him now. Sit down with a beer and quit worrying so much. Okay, Kevin?"

"Yeah, okay. But I'm not going to prison."

Crystal raised her voice. "You won't, Kevin. Just hang in there." She disconnected and called Blake. After four rings, she left a message.

* * *

The detectives and Chuck finished their dessert and retired to the living room. Patty sat across from Chuck. "If you don't mind me asking, were you ever married?"

Chuck stared at the floor and then looked up at Patty. "Yeah. Twice. The first time was just before a six-month deployment in the Marine Corps. I returned home to find my wife pregnant with another guy's child. She was in love with him. They married and moved. I tried again about eight years later. That lasted for ten years. A few years into my SWAT assignment she was offered a job promotion in another state. The prospect of me getting a job in another law enforcement agency with anywhere near the daily action I was experiencing in Boston was non-existent. I look back now and realize that we were each married to our jobs. I decided that working SWAT was not conducive to a stable marriage, so I left that dream. I've had a few girlfriends since then but nothing close to marriage."

CHAPTER 16

Patty walked into the office to find Rick working on a report. "Did you see the newspaper this morning?"

Rick responded without raising his head. "I haven't read it yet."

"There's an article about the barrel of bones found at Ferry Creek Dam. People are pretty concerned."

Rick looked up from his writing. "Well, I guess that's to be expected. It may work in our favor when those responsible for Wellingham's death read about it in the paper."

Patty's phone rang, and she saw that it was Doc Miller.

"Morning, Doc."

"Hi, Patty. How are you and Rick this fine morning?"

"Good, Doc. Rick's friend and former colleague from Boston PD is visiting. I'm getting to know him while he and Rick catch up. What's up with you?"

"Oh, just hanging out here at the morgue as usual. The reason for my call is a suspicious death. Could be nothing, but the death occurred in Brookings, so I'm letting you and Rick know."

"Rick is here, Doc. I'm putting you on speaker phone."

Rick set down his pen. "Hey, Doc."

"Hey, Rick. I'm calling to give you and Patty some work since I'm sure the Barrel Bones case isn't keeping you busy enough."

Rick laughed. "We can always take on more."

"As I mentioned to Patty, this may be nothing, but it's giving me a red flag warning."

"Tell us about it, Doc."

"Two days ago, 911 was called to a Brookings home. The paramedic and EMT who responded found a deceased woman in an upstairs bathroom. There were obvious signs that she'd been quite ill. Considerable vomit and diarrhea. The results of my examination include a slight skin rash, badly scarred liver, and stomach contents that suggest she was poisoned. The husband told the responding officers that he and his wife had spent the morning mushroom-hunting. Upon returning home, she made mushroom soup, ate, and became ill. He said that he offered to drive her to the hospital and that she insisted it was just a twenty-four-hour bug. So he left her and went to his office. Upon returning home, he found her on the bathroom floor. According to him, he then made the emergency call."

"You sound sure that she was poisoned," said Patty. "Any idea what kind of poison?"

"Yes, I am certain she died of mushroom poisoning. I'll have further testing done, but I suspect she ate False Morels, Death Caps, or both."

"Doc," said Rick, "mushroom poisoning happens several times a year due to untrained pickers thinking they know what they're doing. What makes you think this is something more? Something suspicious?"

"Two things, Rick. First, mushroom poisoning that kills takes several hours. The victim experiences excruciating stomach pain, vomiting, and diarrhea. The fact that the husband didn't call for an ambulance earlier in the day, and actually left his ill wife for a time, creates great suspicion for me."

Rick looked at Patty, and she responded to the doc. "That does present a suspicious death. On a scale of one to ten, how convinced are you that this was a criminal act?"

"I'm not the detective, Patty, and I don't know all of the facts, but I'm certain enough that I strongly suggest you and Rick gather the facts you need to fully understand what happened to this woman."

"We'll do that," said Patty. "Thanks for the call. We'll let you know what we find."

"I'd appreciate that. If there is an innocent explanation for all of this, it will be a first for me. You two stay safe."

"Always, Doc," said Rick. "What's the name of the woman?"

"Her name is Bella Lacky. I'll text you her contact information."

Patty wrote down the woman's name. She tapped her pen on her desk. "Why does that woman's name sound familiar?"

"It does to me, too," said Rick.

Patty quit tapping. "I know where we've heard it. Chuck said that the agent he is working with is Kevin Lacky."

"You're right. Could this woman have been Kevin's wife? I'll text Chuck and ask when he last saw Kevin."

Rick sent the text. Two minutes later Chuck responded.

"He's gassing up his truck and on his way here," said Rick. "While we wait for Chuck, I'll find out who responded to the 911 call."

Rick phoned the ambulance service and spoke with the paramedic who was on the call during the evening Bella died.

"Sally, this is Detective Starker. I'm calling about the death of a woman named Bella Lacky. I've got you on speaker phone so that my partner, Detective O'Toole, can participate in this conversation. I understand that you were working that night and got the call."

"I was, Detective, and I won't forget what I saw."

"Would you describe for us everything you can remember?"

"Sure. It's all in my notes. Before I begin, are you thinking this could be something other than a death due to illness?"

"We're investigating all possibilities, Sally. Who was there with Mrs. Lacky when you arrived?"

"Her husband met us at the door and took us upstairs to the bathroom where Mrs. Lacky was lying on the floor."

Patty interrupted before Sally continued. "What was Mr. Lacky's demeanor when he answered the door and let you upstairs?"

"He was exceptionally calm. He said his wife was upstairs in the bathroom and that he'd take us to her. When I saw the state of the woman and the bathroom, it all seemed quite odd."

"What do you mean?" asked Patty.

"Well, the woman was clearly deceased. She was clothed and covered in bloody vomit and excrement. I noticed that the floor looked like someone had tried to clean up the mess."

"What made you think that?" asked Rick.

"Well, there were a couple of soiled towels lying over the side of the bathtub, and areas of the floor looked like they had been wiped with the towels. It was a lot to take in, so I kept my mind on procedure. The officer who arrived on the call about the same time we did, Officer Bradley, phoned our deputy medical examiner and asked that he come to pronounce the woman dead. He spoke to the husband and called the funeral home."

"Did you think about the scene later?" asked Patty.

"I couldn't help but think about it. Part of the reason for it being so difficult to take in was the aloof manner of the husband."

"Okay," said Patty. "Thank you, Sally. We may have more questions."

"I can send you a copy of my report, if that would help."

"Thanks, Sally. That would be helpful."

Patty picked up her cell phone. "Let's talk to Brad and Chuck before I take this to the LT."

Rick got up. "I'll walk down the hall and see if Brad's here."

Rick soon returned. Brad followed with a file in his hand. "Rick says you have some questions relating to the woman who died a few days ago?"

"I do," said Patty. "Her name was Bella Lacky. We have reason to think it's a suspicious death and want to get your input."

"Sure, what can I help with?"

"First," Rick said, "we need the name of the woman's husband."

Brad looked down at his paperwork. "It's Kevin Lacky." He saw Patty glance at Rick. "Do you know him?"

"No, but we know who does."

Patty asked, "What was your impression of the husband when you were there?"

"I remember clearly that he did not act like a guy whose wife had just died a painful death, nor did he seem upset at the horrible scene."

Patty made a few notes while Rick picked up the questioning. "Did he say anything to you?"

"Very little. When I told him his wife was deceased, he asked if I was sure. I responded that I was."

"What did he say to that?"

"He said, 'Okay.' Then he asked what would happen next. I told him that someone from the funeral home would come take his wife from the house and deliver her to the morgue."

"Anything else?" Rick asked.

"Yeah. He asked why she'd be taken to the morgue. I let him know that the medical examiner would need to see her due to the unnatural nature of her death. He then asked what that meant, and I replied that it was highly possible there would be an autopsy. My response seemed to agitate him."

Rick continued with the questions. "What was your impression of the husband's demeanor?"

"He seemed strangely calm. So much so that I wondered if he was in shock. I asked him if there was anyone he could call to stay with him."

Rick made a few notes and looked up. "His response?"

"He said he didn't need anyone. And that he'd be calling a friend after his wife's body was removed."

Patty quit writing. "Were those his exact words, Brad?"

"They were. You two thinking it's a homicide?"

"Could be," said Patty. "Who first responded to the call?"

"Pete did."

"Do you know if he's here today?"

"Yeah. He is. I'll ask him to come talk to you."

"Thanks, Brad."

As Brad left the office, Chuck walked in.

"Hey, Chuck," greeted Rick. "You're just in time to help us out."

"Yeah? What do you need?"

Rick explained the circumstances relating to the death of Bella Lacky. "When's the last time you saw Kevin Lacky?"

"When I wrote up the offer in his office four days ago."

"That," Patty said, "would have been before the death of his wife."

"Is there anything about the guy that might lead you to believe he could have done this?"

"Capable of murdering his wife? There was nothing in the way he acted to suggest he could, but I'm thinking again of what I overheard him say to the broker, Crystal. He said, 'I want her gone' and then 'quid pro quo.' And there is something else I recall. It didn't seem important at the time, but it does now."

"What's that?" asked Rick.

"It was about mushrooms. While Kevin and I were going over the offer, Crystal stepped into his office and told him that she'd spoken with someone, and mushrooms would work."

They all paused to consider how what Chuck had heard related to the death of Bella Lacky.

"I'm taking this to the LT," said Patty. "I think this gives us probable cause for our warrants."

CHAPTER 17

Patty walked down the hall and let the LT know what she and Rick had learned since receiving a call from the medical examiner. "Chuck clearly heard Kevin say he wanted her gone. And he heard Crystal tell Kevin that mushrooms will work. Kevin Lacky's delay in calling for help suggests murder. Crystal's comment about mushrooms suggests that she is a participant in the Bella Lacky death. And we believe she's an accomplice in the murder of her husband. This is probable cause, LT. Rick and I want to investigate Crystal for her participation in the death of Bella Lacky and for the death of Grant Wellingham. Do you find any reason for us not to request a warrant?"

The lieutenant sat back in his chair. "What will you search, and for what reason?"

"We'll search her house, garage, car, home and business computers, and all phones. We'll be looking for anything that ties her to Bella's death by mushrooms and the Barrel Bones murder."

The lieutenant folded his hands on top of his desk. He sat silent for a couple of minutes, a common method of operation for him when pondering decisions. He nodded to Patty. "I agree with you. You have probable cause for a warrant."

Patty smiled. "Thanks, LT." She stood to leave.

"It seems," said the lieutenant, "that Chuck Spencer is now helping you and Rick. He might be able to glean additional information from his real estate agent before escrow closes on the condo."

"I'll suggest that to him, LT. He's let us know that he'd like to help." Patty relayed the lieutenant's message to Rick and Chuck.

Rick smiled as he asked Chuck, "You ready to jump into this?"

"I am. I'll give Kevin Lacky a reason for us to meet after you have your warrant. If he and Crystal are connected, your warrant may push Lacky over the edge."

Patty brought up the template for a search warrant affidavit. "I'll fill out the warrant affidavit now and get it up north before both judges leave for the day." She looked at Rick. "You might want to let Brad and Pete know that if we get our warrant, we'll need them to help out."

"I'll do that," said Rick. "I'd also like to set up an appointment with Bella Lacky's boss after we've acted on the warrant."

"That should be interesting," said Patty as she typed.

An hour later, Patty was sitting in front of one of two Curry County judges. She explained the situation, the reasons why she was requesting the warrant, and specifically the things to which she needed access. The judge concurred. On her way back to Brookings, Patty called Rick.

"We've got it, and I'm just leaving the courthouse. You and Chuck meet me at Crystal's office in thirty minutes. We'll search the office and her car if she's there. Brad and Pete can search the house and any cars she keeps at home. Let them know to bring help. Seize all computers, cell phones, tablets, notebooks, and any other electronic equipment. Let's set the time for entering at two-thirty."

Rick hugged his arm to his gun. "I'll brief Brad and Pete."

"Rick," said Patty, "let's try keeping this quiet. Only those active in the search need to know our plans."

"I agree, and I'll pass that on to the others. Do you want an officer at the back door when we go in?"

"That's a good idea. Pick someone from Patrol."

"Will do."

Chuck had walked down the hall during Patty and Rick's conversation. He brought Brad and Pete back into the office for a briefing from Rick.

Pete stood against the wall. "What's up, Rick?"

"Patty's on her way back from Gold Beach with a warrant. We'll be searching Crystal Wellingham's house, office, garage, and cars. All electronics and cell phones will be seized. Patty wants you and Brad to be lead on the house search. You'll need two more officers for the front and back doors, and whatever you need to keep traffic moving. She wants entry at two-thirty. Can you be ready?"

Both Brad and Pete nodded. "Give us the location of the house. We'll be ready," said Brad. "And I know who we can ask to assist."

Rick opened a drawer at this desk. He thumbed through the file folders, pulled out a form, and handed it to Brad. "Here's the receipt. Make sure to write down everything you remove, regardless of how insignificant it may seem. Take photos of the receipt so that you have a record of proof."

"We've done this before," said Brad. "We know the process."

Rick folded his arms across his chest. "I know you do. But we may have one or more serial killers and, if anyone is guilty, we don't want a technicality interfering with a guilty verdict."

Brad looked down at the form in his hand. "We'll be thorough."

"One more thing. Let's keep this as quiet as possible. Share information only on a need-to-know basis."

Brad looked at Pete and then back to Rick. "Got it."

At two-thirty, Brad and Pete entered Crystal's home. A third officer stood at the back of the house. At one corner of the front of the house, an officer stood where he could watch both the front and side windows. Two patrol officers moved into position, blocking the street at both ends of the block.

Patty, Rick, and Chuck walked into CLW Real Estate. The receptionist quit typing as Patty approached.

"Is Crystal in?"

"Well, yes, she is, but she's with a client and can't be interrupted."

Patty showed her badge to the receptionist. "Please let her know that I need to speak with her now."

The receptionist turned down her lip. "Well, okay. But I was told never to interrupt her when she's with a client." She called Crystal on speed-dial and cringed when Crystal asked the reason for the interruption.

"I'm so sorry, Crystal. But the police are here insisting they talk with you now."

The receptionist looked up at Patty. "Crystal hung up. I'll probably lose my job because of this. I'm a single mom with a five-year-old daughter. What am I going to do now?" Tears began to flow from the young woman's eyes.

Before Patty could respond, she heard Crystal quickly walking down the hall. The sound of her high heels preceded her coming into sight. "What is it you want, Detectives? I'm sorry to be so rude, but I have a business to run. I have clients, and I really don't appreciate your constant interruptions. So unless you have something urgent to discuss, please talk with the receptionist and make an appointment."

Crystal stood in front of Patty with her hands on her hips.

Patty extended her right arm with the warrant in hand. "We have a warrant to search your office and car. This warrant allows us to seize all of your electronic devices, cell phones, and any files we deem to be important relating to the death of Bella Lacky."

Crystal's hands fell to her sides. She then took the warrant from Patty.

Without further hesitation, Patty walked down the hall to Crystal's office. Chuck waited in the reception area, and Rick spoke to the receptionist.

"You don't have to get up, but please roll your chair away from the desk so that I can disconnect the computer and go through the desk drawers."

When Patty began disconnecting Crystal's computer, the client walked out into the entry hall where Crystal was still standing. She noticed the receptionist's tears.

"Crystal, what's going on? Why are the police searching your office?"

Crystal put on a smile and pleaded, "This is all a mistake. I'm so sorry it's happening while you're here. I'll be talking with the police chief and with my attorney. Let me reschedule for a day next week. Would Tuesday afternoon or Thursday morning be best for you?"

The client shook her head in disbelief. "Neither of those days work for me, Crystal. I've changed my mind about listing my home with you. I can't imagine what's going on, but I want no part of it."

Crystal sat down in the reception area and began tapping in Blake's number on her phone. Before the second ring, Patty took Crystal's phone from her hand. Crystal stared up at Patty. "You can't take my phone. I can't make a living without my phone."

"Read the warrant," said Patty.

Crystal unfolded the warrant and began reading the list of those places to be searched. She suddenly turned pale. "This says you can search my house. When do you plan to do this?"

"It's being done right now, Crystal. Your home computers, any cell phones, paper files of interest, garage, and any cars on the premises are being searched as we speak."

"Oh my God. How am I to work?"

Patty ignored the question and called Brad. "Any surprises?"

"No," said Brad. "We've loaded everything from the house, and we'll start back to the station. There is an automobile in the garage that we've not been able to get into. It's locked and we've found no key for it. Do you want to ask Crystal if it's on the keyring she carries with her?"

"Hold on, Brad." Patty walked up to Crystal, who was still sitting in a chair in the reception area, staring at the opposite wall. "I need your keys for the car you have here in the parking lot and the one you keep in your garage at home. I'll return the key to the car in the lot as soon as we have a chance to look inside and in the trunk."

Crystal hesitated, so Patty pointed to the lines on the warrant that provided her with authority to take the keys. This prompted Crystal to stand up. "They're in my purse back in the office. I'll get them for you."

Patty followed Crystal, took the keys, and spoke again on the phone to Brad. "I've got the key you need. We should be done here in about twenty minutes. I'll drop the key off to you on our way back to the station."

Within an hour, all computers, cell phones, tablets, and relevant files from both locations were loaded into the officers' cars. Rick drove to Crystal's house, where Patty gave Brad the key he needed.

At the station, the detectives and Chuck began unloading their vehicle of everything that had been seized.

"Put everything into the extra office," said Patty. "The seized items from the house can be brought into the same room. Then, before we divide up computers and begin searching, we need photos of everything."

While Patty and Rick discussed how to divide up the computers and phones, Chuck called Kevin.

"Kevin, this is Chuck Spencer. I've read through the HOA minutes, and I've found a few concerns about the condo building. I'd like, as soon as possible, to sit down with you and go through my concerns."

"Sure, Chuck. No problem. Work is pretty busy right now. Would Tuesday or Wednesday next week work for you?"

"Next week? Don't you want this to close? We need to work quickly so that I can either cancel the escrow or close per the contract. What are you doing this evening?"

"This evening? Oh, well, okay. Of course I want escrow to close. Let's meet at my office at six."

"You sound rattled, Kevin. Is everything okay with you?"

"Oh, sure. No problem."

"Are you sure? Your voice sounds shaky. Is your wife well?"

"My wife? Well? Yes. I guess I'm just working too hard. I'll see you at six."

Chuck ended the call. Rick and Patty looked up. "I've got a six o'clock appointment at his office. That suggests he doesn't yet know that we've been there."

Brad and Pete arrived at the station with the other patrol officers. Twenty minutes later, Brad walked into the detectives' office and reported to Patty. "Everything is unloaded and stored with the evidence you brought from the real estate office."

"That's great. Now I need you to work with the phones. Print out every phone number that shows up more than once during the last two months. Highlight those numbers for Crystal and Kevin. I'm also interested in any additional numbers that show up on either phone. It will take longer to get the records we need from the service providers, so you'll want to order them ASAP."

Rick and Chuck brought the seized computers back to the detectives' office.

Patty stood up with her coffee cup. "This is going to take a while. Anyone other than me need a bit of fuel?" Both Rick and Chuck handed Patty their cups. She returned with their coffee and went back to the break room for her own and a plate of cookies.

"Oh, yeah," said Rick as he picked up four large chocolate chip cookies. Chuck helped himself, and Patty placed two cookies on a napkin next to her coffee.

"I've got emails here between Crystal and Kevin," said Chuck, "but they all relate to real estate transactions. I'm guessing they were both very careful, and that we'll find communication about the murders only in texts or voice mail messages."

Rick put down a half-eaten cookie and swallowed. "I'm finding the same thing."

The search continued for another couple of hours. Patty sat back in her chair. "It's about six, Chuck. You ready to leave?"

"I am more than ready. I'll take off now and see you in an hour or so."

"Hope it's a fruitful meeting," said Rick. "We need reason to search his house other than the mention of mushrooms."

Chuck put his jacket on. "The conversation might be rough depending upon what Kevin knows about this afternoon. I'll text you both when I leave."

CHAPTER 18

At six, Chuck walked through the front door of CLW and, without waiting, walked back to Kevin's office. He observed that Kevin was the only agent working and that he was visibly upset, nervously scrolling through emails with his finger on the delete button. He stood when Chuck stepped in.

"Oh, Chuck. I didn't hear you come in. How are you this evening?"

Chuck sat down and leaned back comfortably in his chair. "I'm fine, Kevin. How are you?"

Kevin fidgeted with the stapler on his desk, then picked up a pencil to nervously run through his fingers. "Oh, I'm a little tired today. It's been a busy week."

"Seems like you're the only one here today. Some kind of holiday?"

"Uh, no. I guess everyone else is out with clients or done for the day. So what are the questions you have?"

Chuck looked Kevin in the eyes. "I heard your wife died. Is that true?"

Kevin dropped the pencil from his hand. "Where did you hear that?"

"I have friends with the police department. Detectives. They investigate homicides, so they're looking into the death of Grant Wellingham. They also told me that your wife died."

Kevin seemed unable to talk. He closed the top of his computer and looked at Chuck. "Are you a cop?"

"No. Not anymore. I guess my mind still works like one."

"What do you mean by that?"

"I mean that I think you're in some kind of trouble, and that I might be able to help you. I'm wondering why a successful man like yourself would get caught up in a murder investigation."

Kevin's expression turned to fear. "Murder investigation? I don't know what you mean. I'm just a hardworking man. I don't know anything about any murders."

Chuck continued to stare into Kevin's eyes. "You know that earlier today the police raided Crystal's home and her office here. They have her computers and cell phones. The police are, as we speak, matching phone call dates and times on Crystal's phone to your phone."

Kevin was unable to speak, and sweat beads began to form on his forehead.

Chuck leaned forward. "You didn't know?"

Kevin became angry. "You're lying to me. And I can prove it. I'll call Crystal now. She'll explain if anything like that happened."

"Go ahead," said Chuck.

Kevin dialed Crystal's number and waited. After four rings, the phone went to voice mail.

"Crystal, this is Kevin. It is urgent that you give me a call. I'm told that the police searched your office and home. I need to know ASAP what's going on."

Kevin looked at Chuck as if expecting him to call out that he's just joking.

Chuck kept a straight face as he spoke. "She's not going to return your call, Kevin, because the police have her phone. Why did you get mixed up in her problems?"

Kevin grabbed his cell phone and tapped in another number. He looked up at Chuck. "I have another way to confirm you're wrong." A recorded message intercepted the rings at the other end of the phone line. "You have reached a disconnected number." Kevin hung up before listening to the entire recording. He looked at the cell phone in his hand. "I must have dialed wrong." He tried again with the same outcome.

Chuck leaned forward. "Why did you do it, Kevin? Did she coerce you into working with her? Did she threaten to harm you financially if you didn't kill her husband? Why?"

Kevin looked dazed. "I didn't kill him." He looked at his cell phone. "He did. He said no one would ever know."

"Who, Kevin? Who killed Grant Wellingham? Are this other guy and Crystal trying to pin the murder on you?"

Kevin lowered his eyebrows and seemed to have shaken off the initial shock of hearing the recording on Blake's phone number. He looked at Chuck. "I'm not talking to you anymore. I need to go home. I need to think about all of this."

"This is not something you can walk away from, Kevin." Chuck sent a quick text to Patty and Rick letting them know that Kevin admitted Grant Wellingham was murdered by someone he knew. "It's best for you, Kevin, if we wait for Detectives O'Toole and Starker. They'll be here in a few minutes."

Kevin closed his computer, stood up, and put the computer under his arm. "You can't make me stay here."

"You're right, Kevin. I can't. But you just revealed that you know Mr. Wellingham was murdered and by whom. That's life in prison, Kevin. The sentence might be different if you explain that you were coerced or black-mailed. Is that what happened?"

Kevin looked at Chuck with a defeated expression. "It's Crystal they want. Not me. I'm going home."

Chuck heard sirens in the distance. He moved out of the way and allowed Kevin to exit his office and walk toward the front door.

"They're here, Kevin."

Kevin opened the front door to see Detectives O'Toole and Starker walking toward the real estate building. He stepped back in and shut the door.

Two minutes later, Rick handcuffed Kevin. "We're arresting you for the murder of Bella Lacky."

Kevin stared out the window of the police car as Rick drove to the station. "I don't know how I got caught up in all of this. I worked hard to make life good for Bella and me. But she didn't care. I don't think she ever loved me.

Crystal always acted like she cared about me. She helped me get my business going. She assured me everything would be okay."

Kevin saw Patty looking at him by way of the rear-view mirror. "It was always Crystal's idea. And Blake's. After helping her out the first time, it got easier. We were just eliminating the problems in our lives."

The interview room was small and allowed room for a table and three chairs. Kevin walked in looking at his reflection in the mirror. The detectives sat at the opposite side of the table. Chuck stood in an adjoining room, watching the interview through the mirrored window. He turned on the speaker allowing him to hear the conversation.

Patty asked Kevin to sit down in the chair facing the mirror. "Detective Starker and I need to take care of something. You need to wait here. We'll return shortly."

Patty and Rick returned to their desks. "Let's give him forty minutes," said Patty. "Maybe he'll be ready to tell us more."

Rick made a few notes on the yellow tablet in front of him. "He's admitted to being involved with the Barrel Bones murder, and he mentioned a third person: Blake."

Patty sipped water from a pink polka-dot water bottle on her desk. "After sitting alone for this long, I'm hoping he'll tell us a lot more before we have to admonish him."

When the detectives returned to the interview room and sat down at the table, they silently stared at Kevin, waiting for him to speak.

Kevin looked around the room a few times as though searching for some way out of the mess he was in. He fidgeted and rubbed his hands on his thighs, attempting to remove the sweat.

"She said it would be easy. Blake said there was no way for the police to ever identify Grant and, therefore, no way to charge us. I don't know how it all went wrong. But they are the ones you want to arrest. I just helped Blake move the barrel in and out of his truck and into the reservoir. I had nothing to do with cutting up the body. I couldn't do that kind of thing. Too gruesome." He paused long enough for Rick to stand up.

"I'm going to get a glass of water. Would you like one, Kevin?"

Kevin leaned back in his chair. "Is that all you're going to say? I just told you that it was Crystal and Blake who murdered Grant, and all you can do is ask if I want water?" He waited for a response.

Patty remained silent while Rick asked again. "Water, Kevin?"

Kevin moved closer to the edge of the table. "Yeah, yeah, okay."

Rick left the room and stood outside the two-way window with Chuck while one of the other officers went for the waters. Patty continued to sit quietly, waiting for Kevin to go on. And he did.

"You have to believe me, Detective, when I tell you that the murder wasn't my fault. Crystal just couldn't stand the idea of Grant getting half of her business, so she explained that Blake would commit the murder. All I had to do was help. She knew I could do what she'd asked since I'd helped her once before. My part wasn't really a big deal."

Rick walked back into the room with three glasses of water and set them on the table. He glanced at Patty and remained standing. Patty stood up and asked Rick to step into the hall with her. He did and held the door open as Patty whispered, "He's helped Crystal before."

"I heard," said Rick.

"We may have more than two murders."

Rick then intentionally spoke loud enough for Kevin to hear. "Death Cap mushrooms. Dead before the 911 call."

"That should do it," whispered Patty.

The two detectives returned to the table and sat down across from Kevin.

Kevin leaned forward with his elbows on the table and hands outstretched. "I would have called 911 sooner, but Blake told me to wait. And Crystal thought everything would be okay. I would not have done anything if she hadn't told me everything would be okay. She's the one you want. Her and Blake."

Kevin waited again for a response from the detectives. "This is bad, isn't it? Well, I didn't agree to go to prison for Crystal. I'll tell you anything you want to know. I just don't want to go to prison." He folded his hands on top of the table and put his head down on them. He murmured, "I'll tell you what you want to know in exchange for you not sending me to prison."

Patty and Rick waited for Kevin to say more. After a few minutes of silence,

Patty nodded to Rick and then spoke to Kevin. "Kevin, we've listened to you, and we believe that you don't want to go to prison. We have a few questions, but first Detective Starker will read you your rights."

Rick pulled a small Miranda card from his pocket and read, "You have the right to remain silent. Anything you say can and will be used against you in a court of law. You have the right to talk to a lawyer and have him present with you while you are being questioned. If you cannot afford to hire a lawyer, one will be appointed to represent you before any questioning if you wish. You can decide at any time to exercise these rights and not answer any questions or make any statement." He put the card back in his pocket and looked at Kevin. "Do you understand each of these rights?"

Kevin nodded. "Yeah." He raised his head from his hands. "But wait a minute. You were supposed to tell me those rights as soon as I came into the room. Before I said anything about Crystal and Blake. Now you can't arrest me."

Patty quietly explained how Miranda works. "We were not yet questioning you, Kevin. You see, there are three conditions that must be in place before we are required to read you your rights. The first is that you have to be in a position where you can't voluntarily leave."

"I am."

"That's right, Kevin. The second action is that we suspect you of committing a specific crime."

"And you do. You think I killed Bella. What's the third thing?"

"The third is that we are asking questions specifically about the criminal action for which we believe you are guilty."

"Okay. So why wasn't Detective Starker supposed to read that card when I first came in?"

"He didn't read it because we were not yet asking questions. We were simply listening."

Rick put the Miranda card back into his pocket and asked, "So it was Crystal who got you involved in all of the murders? You are telling us that you played a minor role. Is that true? If it is true, you may not have a lot to worry about."

Kevin furrowed his eyebrows and pursed his lips. "You don't think so?"

Patty spoke softly. "We are just trying to clarify our understanding of what you've already said. Do you understand what I'm saying? You want us to try and lessen your sentence because of what you're saying your role was in the murders, and we just want to clarify our understanding."

"Yeah, okay. I guess I can clarify anything I've already said."

Patty glanced at Rick and then continued, "You are saying that the murders were Crystal's idea. Crystal and Blake?"

"Yeah. That's right."

"Who's Blake, Kevin? We will need to confirm that he's a real person and not just some name you're giving us."

Kevin rubbed the palms of his hands on his thighs again. "All I know is that his name is Blake. I don't have a last name for him."

"What about an address?" asked Patty.

Kevin slowly shook his head. "I've never had one. I don't know where he lives. I've never been to his house."

"How did you communicate with this Blake?"

"He called me, or I called him. It wasn't a lot because he didn't like dealing with anyone but Crystal."

"Will you be able to pick out Blake's phone number on your phone call record?"

"Yeah. I can do that."

"That's very helpful, Kevin," said Patty. "You mentioned murders. What are the names of the victims?"

Kevin looked confused. "Names of victims? I thought you knew who had died."

"We know that Grant Wellingham was murdered. And that your wife Bella died of mushroom poisoning. It's looking more and more like you are responsible for her death."

Kevin opened his eyes wide. "Responsible for her death? You have no evidence to pin that on me."

"Well," said Patty, "that isn't exactly true. You see, earlier this morning a search warrant was granted for us to search your home, office, computers, and the cell phone that I am taking from you now. You said that you spoke with Blake, and we know there are messages between you and Crystal. We will find evidence, Kevin, that ties you to the two murders and possibly more."

"My condo? Oh, please don't mess up my home. I only just finished cleaning the bathroom after Bella, you know, died. She left an awful mess."

Patty softened her voice. "Tell us more about Blake's role in the murders."

Kevin looked around the room. "Oh, God. This is all so wrong." He looked at Patty. "You can't pin Bella's death on me. She died of mushroom poisoning. You know that. She picked the mushrooms. She made the soup. Then, when I wanted to call for help, she told me not to. Her death is not my fault."

Patty continued to look Kevin in the eyes. She spoke quietly. "We know all of that, Kevin. Maybe she accidentally put the poisonous mushrooms in to her soup, or maybe you added them. Your problem is that you waited to call 911 until after your wife was dead. We know that death from mushroom poisoning is excruciatingly painful, and that death can take six or more hours. You could have saved her, Kevin, and you chose to let her die."

Kevin looked down at the table.

Rick suddenly slapped his hand on the table and demanded that Kevin respond. "Did you put the poisonous mushrooms in your wife's soup, Kevin? Is that why you didn't save her? Was it your intent that she die?"

Kevin jumped at the noise of Rick's hand slapping the table. He now looked frantic. "I am not the guilty one here. She is. Crystal is. I'm not saying anything else."

Patty spoke again in her soft voice. "Just answer one more question, Kevin. Who was the third victim?"

Kevin looked up at Patty, still stunned by Rick's aggressive approach.

"A third victim?"

"Yes," said Patty. "You mentioned that there had been a murder prior to the murder of Grant Wellingham. Was that your first murder?"

Kevin stood up and began pacing the floor.

"We need for you to sit down, Kevin," said Patty.

Kevin stopped pacing and looked at the detectives. "I want an attorney."

CHAPTER 19

Crystal bought a burner phone and called Blake on the number he'd given her. Blake didn't recognize the caller's number and let it go to voice mail. At the sound of the tone, Crystal left a message. "Call me as soon as you get this message."

Blake picked up the message and made the call. "What now, Crystal? And why the new phone number? I'm busy."

"Shut up, Blake, and listen. The police came into my office with a search warrant. They've seized my computers and cell phone. This is a burner." Crystal listened for a response. Hearing none, she continued. "Are you there, Blake?"

"Yeah, Crystal, I'm here. You're in trouble because of that scumbag you insisted on helping. I told you to keep him out of it. So now, just keep your mouth shut and let the cops search. They can't prove you were involved with Grant's death."

"Well, Blake, that's not our only problem. Kevin's office and home were also searched, and he's been arrested."

"Arrested! Why?"

"I don't know yet. I haven't been able to talk with Kevin. The cops have his cell phone and computers. Your prior number is on his cell phone. They are questioning Kevin now. This is bad, Blake."

Blake yelled a series of expletives at Crystal. "You were so stupid, Crystal.

Everything was going well until you got wrapped up in helping that guy. Have you had something on the side with him, Crystal? Is that it? I've never known you to let personal needs get in the way of business."

"No, Blake. It's never been anything like that. And you're right, as always. I was stupid to think I could help him out. It's just that he knows what we've done, and I figured helping him would keep him quiet."

"Well, it's not going to keep him quiet now, Crystal."

"I don't know what to do, Blake. I'll talk with my divorce attorney and ask who I should go to with this."

"Just keep your mouth shut, Crystal. Don't tell your attorney anything until I tell you to. I'll take care of our problem."

"Okay, Blake. I'll be quiet."

CHAPTER 20

It was one of those mornings in Brookings when the fog reduces visibility to a couple hundred feet. The weather prediction is in the low sixties, but the fog lowers that number by about ten degrees.

Rick and Patty were finishing up their search on the computers belonging to Crystal and Kevin. Chuck was reviewing file notes.

"I've got it!" Rick called out. "A history of poisonous mushrooms, including the Death Cap and False Morel. I'm surprised he did his research on his business laptop."

Patty looked up. "Not too bright. But then we know that. Now we need something specific tying Kevin to his wife's death."

"Once again," said Rick, "there doesn't seem to be much in the way of emails."

"I gave his cell phone to Brad and Pete to work with. They'll be cross-checking numbers with Crystal's phone and looking for text messages. On a personal note, I'm starving. How about I order pizza? Pepperoni and cheese? Anyone for mushrooms?"

Chuck smiled. "Sure, seems more than appropriate for this investigation."

Twenty minutes later, the pizza arrived. Chuck walked down the hall to invite Brad and Pete into the break room. Patty opened the boxes. "I think there's something for everyone. There's even anchovies on half of the pep-peroni and cheese for you, Pete."

"Thanks, Patty. Nothing like a little brain and heart health to go with the pepperoni."

Brad took a step back. "Anchovies for brain and heart health? What kind of doctor are you seeing?"

Pete responded in a matter-of-fact way. "Anchovies have many vitamins and minerals. They are best known as a source of Omega-3 fatty acids. And Omega-3 fatty acids promote brain and heart health."

"Wow," said Brad. "I didn't know that."

Pete smiled. "I rest my case."

Brad shook his head as everyone else enjoyed the ribbing. "Okay. You've had your fun. I'm taking the last piece of pepperoni."

Patty moved her plate to the side and opened the file she'd brought in. "This is a working feed. Now that we've all served ourselves, let's go around the circle and contribute what we know about the murders of Grant Wellingham and Bella Lacky."

Rick sat down last with three pieces of pizza on his paper plate. "I'll start. On the Barrel Bones case we've got identification of the victim, Grant Welling-ham. He was killed by being stabbed with an instrument that pierced his heart. He was then dismembered and placed in a lye solution within a closed barrel. Grant was married to Crystal Wellingham, broker-owner of CLW Real Estate.

"Kevin Lacky is one of the agents and, it seems, a participant in Grant's murder, though he claims his role was minor. Nonetheless, we've got him on that verbal admission and on waiting until after his wife was dead before dialing 911. He's told us that there is someone named Blake who is a partner in at least one of the murders. Kevin doesn't have a last name for Blake, nor does he know where the guy lives. Kevin's use of the word 'murders' in the plural suggests that, in addition to his involvement with the murders of both Wellingham and Kevin's late wife Bella, there could be a third."

Brad swallowed the cheese and pepperoni in his mouth before speak-ing. "Pete and I have listed every number found on the phones of Crystal and Kevin for the past two years. The numbers represent calls out and calls received. So far, we've found numerous calls between Crystal and Kevin. We've also found a few calls on Kevin's phone to a number that also shows up several times over the past couple of months on Crystal's phone. Information from the cell phone servers should be here tomorrow."

"And," said Pete, "in addition to the called/received numbers, we checked the contacts on both Crystal and Kevin's phones. There is no contact associated with the third number. It could belong to the guy, Blake, that Kevin mentioned."

Patty looked at Chuck for him to go next.

"Kevin has stated several times that Crystal is the one behind the murders. I believe he provided the poison mushrooms that killed his wife, but we don't yet have proof. I have an idea on how to find the guy Kevin mentioned. I'll talk about that after Patty tells us more about what is known."

Patty set her plate aside and used a napkin to get the tomato sauce off her fingers before speaking. "Crystal refuses to talk with us. Kevin maintains that Crystal was involved in both Grant and Bella's murders, but we don't have anything solid yet that we can use as a basis for her arrest. Kevin is breaking and gave us some helpful information before demanding his right to counsel. He believes Crystal will hang him out to dry, and he wants to make a deal to keep himself from going to prison, but he hasn't yet told us exactly what it is he has to offer. He seems to be afraid of the guy named Blake. I think we should arraign him and ask for bail. Let's see who, if anyone, posts it for him."

"That works for me," said Rick, followed by nods from the others.

Patty looked at Chuck. "You have an idea for finding the missing Blake?"

Chuck set his coffee cup down. "I do. Geofencing."

Rick raised his eyebrows. "I've read about that."

"I have too," said Patty. "But I've never given it much thought since we've had no need. Tell us how this might work."

"Give me a minute to refill my mug."

Chuck returned and set down his coffee. "Geofencing is a method of locating someone using cell phone towers, radio frequency identification, GPS, Wi-Fi, or cellular data. It can be used to advertise, to send subliminal messages, or, in our case, to search for someone. It's a type of reverse warrant.

"A geofence is a virtual boundary created around a geographical location using Google geofence and cellular 'Tower Dump' technology. Geofencing has become an essential tool for law enforcement agencies in investigating and solving crimes."

Patty interrupted. "How is this not an invasion of privacy?"

"That is a consideration still being discussed within our legal system. It is legal for use by law enforcement provided we have a warrant for the search. And that's something I can help you with."

Pete cleared his throat. "This is all new to me. So how will this help us to locate the missing third accomplice in the murders?"

"Good question," said Chuck. "We can start by tracking the phone number you and Brad found on both Crystal and Kevin's phones. The use of the number is recent enough that we can use geofencing technology to locate a geographic area from where the calls were made."

Chuck looked at Patty, and she responded with interest. "Keep going, Chuck. This is great."

"A geofence warrant is issued by the court to allow law enforcement to search a database to find all active mobile devices within a particular geofence area. We'll start by completing an affidavit for the geofence warrant. I'll work with Patty on that. It's a three-stage warrant process that is based upon an agreement between Google and the Department of Justice's Computer Crime and Intellectual Property. After receiving the warrant, we'll send it to Google. Once Google receives it, they will take on an extrajudicial role of determining whether we have complied with a probable cause search."

Patty looked at Rick and then back to Chuck. "How will Google know the geographic area to search? We can't have them looking throughout the entire state."

"You're right, Patty, we have to define parameters. And we'll do that with zip codes. We know that the elusive third person we're hoping to find probably lives within a two-hour driving distance from Brookings. So, to start with, we'll provide zip codes for several areas including Del Norte and Humboldt counties in California and Curry, Coos, and Josephine counties here in Oregon. Google will provide us with a list of dates and times during which that number was used. Google has been able to provide not only the account subscriber's name but also the email account and username associated with the number."

"What if the phone used was a burner phone?" asked Brad. "Can it still be tracked?"

"Another good question, and the answer is 'possibly.' I don't know enough to give you a more detailed response. But Google's experts will."

Patty looked around the room. "You guys have any more questions?" She looked at Chuck. "That's great information. It's exactly what we now need for this case." She stood up, walked over to the window, and looked out at the young kids riding bikes. "We have to remove these murderers from our community. And unless we get a full confession from one of the three suspects, we need the lye or the murder weapon. Tying the murders to Crystal and the others is crucial." She looked at Chuck. "Let's complete that affidavit, and you can give me instruction as to where to send it."

CHAPTER 21

The day started off with an offshore fog bank and the promise of sun by afternoon, something coastal residents are used to. Rick and Patty arrived at work about the same time. Red lights blinked on their desk phones.

Patty took her jacket off and hung it over the back of her chair. "There was a time when all we had were landlines. We expected the blinking light and lots of messages. But it seems a little outdated nowadays, when the great majority of our calls are on cell phones."

"Like something from the past," said Rick. He turned toward the door. "I'm going for a refill and to look for cookies. You ready for coffee?"

Patty gave Rick her coffee cup. "Coffee will be great, but I don't need any cookies."

While Rick was on the coffee run, Patty listened to her messages. She hung up after the second one and called the jail. Rick walked in and heard Patty's side of the conversation.

"When? Who posted bail? What's his address? Okay, thanks."

Rick set Patty's coffee on her desk, sat down, and began enjoying his morning fuel. He knew Patty was talking with the jail and waited for her to fill him in on the call.

Patty hung up the phone and shook her head in disbelief. "Bail was posted early this morning for Kevin."

Rick swallowed his coffee. "Who bailed him out?"

"The guy named Blake. Last name, Cirelli. His driver's license shows a Cave Junction address. The license expires in eight months, so there's a possibility he no longer lives there."

"We need to find out," said Rick.

"I agree. I'll run his name and see if he has any priors."

Rick texted Chuck.

"He's in here," Patty said, "but only for petty theft."

"Maybe he's graduated. I just sent a text to Chuck asking if he's coming in this morning."

"I want to let the LT know what's happened. We need to take a drive to Cave Junction."

Rick's phone vibrated. "It's Chuck. Shall I ask him to join us on the trip?"

Patty started for the door. "He'd be good to have along."

Down the hall, Patty approached the lieutenant's office. The lieutenant looked up and through the open venetian blinds. "Good morning, O'Toole."

"Good morning, LT."

"Here to talk about your bailed suspect?"

Patty tried to hide her surprise. The lieutenant seemed to hear everything within the department before she and Rick did. "I am, LT. The guy who posted bail for Kevin is, we believe, the third accomplice to the murders of Wellingham and Lacky. We also suspect he may be the one who killed Wellingham before Kevin assisted with the lye treatment and transporting barrel up to the Ferry Creek dam. The suspect's name is Blake Cirelli. His driver's license shows a Cave Junction address. Rick, Chuck, and I will drive out there today to either arrest Cirelli or get a handle on where he might be."

"Good idea, O'Toole. You going to get a couple deputies to help?"

"We hope to. I'll call Josephine County's sheriff before we leave."

"Well, be careful. If this is the guy who killed Wellingham and cut him into pieces, he's dangerous. Most likely a sociopath."

"Thanks, LT. We agree. Kevin Lacky seems to be afraid of Blake, and yet he told Chuck several times that the murders are Crystal and Blake's fault.

Someone's being manipulated. We just haven't figured out whether it's Blake or Crystal pulling the strings."

The lieutenant sat back in his chair. "Keep me updated."

"Will do, LT."

Patty returned to her desk and found that Chuck had arrived. "The LT agrees with our trip to Cave Junction and warned us all to be careful, calling Blake, if he's guilty, a sociopath."

"He could also be a psychopath," said Chuck. "One or the other, he's one bad dude."

"Before we leave, I'll call Josephine County." Patty typed on her keyboard and brought up a list of numbers on the computer. She tapped one into her phone. It rang twice before the call was answered by dispatch. "This is Detective Patty O'Toole with Brookings PD. Is the sheriff available?" Thirty seconds later, Patty greeted the sheriff. "Thanks, Sheriff. Good to talk with you, too. It has been a while and I feel kind of bad letting you know that we believe another suspected murderer may be living in your county." She smiled. "Yeah, I guess so." She went on to explain the reason for the call. "Any chance you can help us out with a couple deputies when we arrive at the target house? Thanks. I'm hoping they won't be necessary, but I appreciate your help."

Patty ended the call and stood up to leave. "Sheriff says he'll have two deputies meet us at the corner about a block from the target house. He gave me the street names. Any questions before we go?"

"I have a concern," said Rick. "Why would Blake bail Kevin out? Why not let him sit in jail?"

"Blake's scared Kevin will talk," said Chuck.

"I'm beginning to think the same thing," said Rick. "Blake knows that Kevin is the weak link in the group."

"And we know that too," said Patty. "Kevin's already given us enough to put Crystal away. If Blake is the cold-blooded killer we think he is, what's to stop him from taking out Kevin? Let's have Kevin located and an officer watch him until we can get him to court."

"I'll see if Brad and Pete are still here," said Rick.

Rick walked down the hall and returned with the two officers. "I've let them know that Kevin was bailed out this morning."

Patty looked at Brad. "We need Kevin Lacky found before Blake or Crystal decides Kevin needs to go away permanently. Put a BOLO out and take Pete with you to Kevin's condo. If he's not there, try the CLW offices."

Brad shook his head. "What do you want us to do if we find him?"

"Sit on him for as long as you can. Let him know of our concern for his safety. Tell him to stay clear of Blake. Rick, Chuck, and I are on our way to Cirelli's address in Cave Junction. Stay in touch with me. If we lose cell service while on our phones, I'll call back when we have service again."

Patty put her purse in her lower desk drawer. "Okay, guys. Let's go now. It will take us about an hour and a half to get there. The deputies will meet us at four. It's two now, so we'll have a little extra time in the event there's road work on 199."

Rick picked up his keys and looked at Patty. "Did you want to take the wheel this trip so that I can enjoy the flora and fauna along the way?"

Patty paused, touched her forehead, and looked as though she was giving the question a lot of thought. "I don't think so. Not this trip."

Chuck looked at Rick and then at Patty. "I feel left out. Was something going on there?"

Patty smiled. "Just a little partner humor."

Once on the road, Chuck leaned forward from the back seat so that Rick and Patty could hear him. "I got an email this morning from a guy I worked with. His sixteen-year-old neighbor shot an intruder breaking into their home. The kid was awakened by noise in their living room, grabbed his rifle, and went to check. The intruder was just lowering his second leg into the room when he saw the kid and pulled a knife. The kid shot twice. The first shot took out an eye and the second pierced one lung. The mayor's already recognized the kid as a hero and announced an annual day of recognition for the kid and the right to protect oneself and one's property."

Patty looked in the rear-view mirror at Chuck. "Incidents like that are always good to hear, Chuck. Too bad the mainstream media doesn't publicize them."

"They're not made public because a large percentage of mainstream media doesn't want the public to know that studies show firearms are used more than two million times a year for personal protection, and that the presence of a firearm, without a shot being fired, prevents crime in many instances."

"This situation resulted in lives saved," said Rick, "but it could have gone south if the kid didn't know the law. Gun owners should be educated about their rights. Shooting can be justified, but only where crime constitutes an imminent threat to life, limb, or, in some cases, property."

"Maybe," said Patty, "we should offer a few classes to the public about gun safety and citizens' rights."

"That's a good idea. You can discuss that with the LT and get his input on what we might do after we solve the two murder cases we're working."

"All in good time."

Chuck noticed the burned areas on both sides of the river. "Looks like you had quite a fire out here."

"Yeah," said Rick. "They seem to happen more frequently in recent years than I recall a decade ago. The starter for the most part has been lightning, something over which we have no control. Fires are always a threat in this area."

"That reminds me, Chuck," said Patty. "With your trips back and forth to Brookings, always check the status of Highway 199. You may need to drive north on Highway 101 rather than 5. There are some benefits of driving 101. You can eat lunch at The Peg House in Leggett, where their slogan is *Never Don't Stop*. Further north you'll have a good chance of seeing elk while passing the Elk Country RV Park. Last time I drove that route, I had to stop on the highway to let a couple of them cross."

"Thanks for the tip, Patty. I may drive 101 next trip just to see what you've described."

Patty looked at Chuck in the rear-view mirror. "How is your escrow proceeding since Kevin was arrested?"

"We're moving forward without a problem. I'm working with the title officer and the seller's agent. I've removed all of my contingencies, and the bank is ready to fund. I expect to close next week."

"That's great," said Rick. "We should all go out to Dewy's and celebrate your receipt of the keys to your new home on the ocean."

Chuck agreed. "I look forward to it."

Patty's phone chimed and she saw that it was Brad. "Hey, Brad. What? Hello? Hello?" Patty waited for a response. "Dang. The call dropped. I'll call him back when we pick up service. I did hear him say that he has bad news."

A passing lane opened up, and Rick pulled out from behind a pickup and trailer. "We're not too far from O'Brien, where you'll have service again. If need be, I can pull over while you call Brad."

"That would be good." The atmosphere in the car became one of quiet contemplation until Patty was able to get through to Brad. Rick pulled over.

"Hey, Brad. I've got you on speaker phone. What have you got?"

"Someone tried to kill Kevin about two hours ago. He was walking from his car to his condo building. A guy on a bicycle passed Kevin and knifed him in the side. A neighbor stepped out of his front door, saw Kevin hit the ground, and took off after the guy on the bike. He scared the guy off and then called 911. The knife pierced Kevin's spleen. He's at Curry General getting patched up."

Patty paused and then responded with concern. "We need someone posted outside of Kevin's hospital room at all times. No one other than medical personnel should be allowed in. Can you take care of that?"

"No problem, Patty. I'll get someone over there right away. I'll set up shifts."

"Thanks, Brad. We'll go straight to the hospital when we get back."

Rick pulled back out onto the highway. "Seems someone wanted to scare Kevin rather than kill him."

"Or," said Chuck, "they hired the wrong guy to do the job."

The detectives and Chuck met with two Josephine County deputies at the time and place Patty and the sheriff had discussed. Patty went over the plan. "Rick and I will go to the front door. Chuck can go around back." Patty looked at the deputies. "You two take the front and any side windows. We don't know whether our suspect will be here, but if he is, we want him alive."

"Understood," said a deputy. "If he puts up a fight, we can call a couple of reserves to manage traffic."

"That's good," said Patty.

The house was one of several on a narrow street. It had a quaint look about it because of the long front porch and picket fence. Patty and Rick climbed quietly up the five steps to the porch and front door. Rick knocked. After a short wait, a middle-aged woman opened the door.

"Yes?"

Patty stepped forward. "I'm Detective O'Toole and this is Detective Starker. Does Blake Cirelli live here?"

The woman at the door hesitated and squinted her eyes. "Why do you want to know?"

Patty was careful with how she approached the woman. "We're detectives from Brookings investigating a homicide. We have reason to believe that Blake has information that will help us. Is he here?"

The woman stared above the detectives and into the sky. She brought her eyes down to Patty's. "He isn't living here right now. I think he has a girlfriend and is living with her. He only occasionally stops here to say hi."

"I see," said Patty. "What is your name?"

"Why do you need to know that?"

Patty smiled. "It would be nice to call you by name, and to know if you're a relative or a neighbor."

"Oh, okay. My name is Tina. I'm Blake's sister."

Patty smiled. "Tina, it's nice to meet you. Do you know where Blake's girlfriend lives?"

"I don't know exactly, but I think she lives in Smith River or Crescent City."

"Smith River or Crescent City," Patty repeated. "And her name?"

"I've heard him talk about a Kelly, but I don't know if that's his current girlfriend and, before you ask, I don't know her last name."

"Thank you, Tina. You've been helpful. If Blake shows up, will you please let him know that we'd like his help? And if you think of something more that might help us find him, please give me a call." Patty handed the woman her business card.

"Sure. I'll tell him."

Patty and Rick left the house and walked back to the deputies and Chuck.

"He's not here. I'll ask the sheriff if his deputies can keep an eye on this house in the event Blake returns. Let's get back to Brookings."

The conversation was light during the return drive. "Well," said Patty, "we know a little more than we did. He has stayed local."

"The geofencing will help us out," said Chuck. "Being out here in rural America, I've been wondering how a sheriff handles crimes taking place in several areas at once without adequate staffing."

"Well, in some counties the sheriff has a posse, historically called a 'posse comitatus.'"

"I've read a little about them," said Rick.

"We had no need in Boston. So, Patty, tell me more about the posse comitatus."

"There's not a lot I can tell you. It is a group mobilized by the sheriff to suppress lawlessness in the county. Like in a western classic film. Historically, the posse movement grew slowly in Oregon. One group registered its charter in Lane County in 1973 and, a year later, according to FBI investigators, established the first citizens' grand jury in the nation. The posse is overseen by the county sheriff and must all be civilians. Soldiers are prohibited from participating."

"That's interesting," said Chuck. "I can see how such a group would be helpful to a sheriff with a small number of deputies relative to the area served. I wonder if our sheriff has one for Curry County?"

"The members of a posse comitatus, or posse, can also be used for search and rescue. Our sheriff does have a Search and Rescue division and therefore probably has a posse even if he doesn't address the volunteers as such."

CHAPTER 22

It was evening when Rick pulled into the parking lot of Curry General Hospital. Patty and Rick showed their badges at the front desk. Chuck gave the receptionist his retired law enforcement business card. They took the elevator to the third floor and found Pete sitting on a chair next to the door of Kevin's room. He stood up and put his book down on the chair. "Hey, guys. No action here. Just nurses and doctors entering the room."

"How long have you been here?" asked Patty.

"Since four. Brad has us working six-hour shifts."

"Thanks, Pete. Maybe we'll find out who did this."

Kevin was awake. Rick and Chuck remained at the door while Patty spoke to the injured murder suspect. "Did you see who stabbed you, Kevin?"

Kevin stirred. His eyelids drooped due to medication. He looked up at Patty. "No. It all happened too fast. Some guy on a bike. I thought at first that he'd just bumped into me until I grabbed my side and saw the blood. Then I passed out."

"It was your neighbor who chased the guy away. We are concerned that the guy on the bike may have intended to kill rather than maim you. Any ideas on who would do this?"

Kevin blinked his eyes. "Probably Blake. He was angry when he bailed me out of jail this morning. He called me a rat. And when he dropped me off at home, he said I'd better disappear if I knew what was good for me."

"Did you respond when he said that?"

"Yeah. I told him that this is my home and I'm not going anywhere."

"If this was Blake's doing, Kevin, we're worried he'll have someone finish the job. You've been safe while in this room because we have an officer stationed outside your door. But the hospital will discharge you in the next couple of days. We can help you if you help us. What was Blake's role in the murders?"

Kevin's eyes slowly closed when his nurse walked into the room. "That's enough for now, Detectives. He needs rest, and I'm about to give him a little more pain medication so that he can sleep."

Patty looked at Rick and then the nurse. "Okay. We'll come back in the morning."

Pete closed his book when Patty stepped out.

"How long before you go home?" Patty asked.

"I've got another three hours."

"You want anything? Coffee? Cafeteria food?"

"Thanks, but the nurses have been taking good care of me. They brought me a burger, fries, and a Coke about an hour ago."

Chuck put his hand on his stomach. "That sounds good. Maybe I should take a shift."

Pete smiled. "Let Brad know. I'm sure he can fit you in."

* * *

Thirty minutes later, the detectives and Chuck were in Patty and Rick's office. Patty and Rick shut down their computers.

"Before leaving, I'm going to call Crystal and ask if she'll come in tomorrow to answer a few questions about her husband's death. Maybe she'll figure it's in her best interest to cooperate. Any objection to our going out to eat after that?" Patty asked.

"Good idea," said Rick. "How about you, Chuck?"

"I'm in."

Dinner was casual and quiet. When the server arrived for the drink order, Patty ordered a Chardonnay, Chuck a draft, and Rick a Coke. Chuck perused his menu and then looked up at Rick. "I've noticed that you haven't had an alcoholic drink since I arrived. Something recent?"

"I've been sober for about six years now. You remember how I was when Claire and Skylar were murdered?"

Chuck looked at Patty. "It was bad." He then turned to Rick. "There were a couple of times when I wasn't sure you'd make it to retirement."

Rick fidgeted with the menu. "Yeah, I wasn't sure either. I moved out here figuring the low crime rate, minimal traffic, and fresh air were all that I needed to get well."

Chuck nodded. "Until they weren't all you needed."

"Right. We had an incident that brought back my trauma with their deaths. I started leaning on the alcohol to be able to sleep at night."

"What got you to stop?"

Rick turned toward Patty. "She did."

Patty reached out and put a hand on Rick's shoulder. "He just needed encouragement."

Rick looked pensively around the room. "Or an ultimatum."

Chuck looked at the concerned look on Patty's face. "Tough call."

"It was," said Patty. "And Rick understood why."

"Anyway," said Rick, "I went to AA meetings for a couple of years and found that life for me is much easier without alcohol. Since then, it's been one day at a time and trying to make the most of each of them. I found happiness again here, with Patty."

Patty looked into Rick's eyes. "That goes both ways."

The server brought drinks and took their orders. Chuck gathered up the menus and handed them to her. "Well, Patty, it's clear to me that Rick is happier than he's been in a long while. It's also clear that you care deeply for each other. Any plans for the future?"

The couple looked at each other. "We've come close a couple of times, but something has always interrupted our planning."

"Yeah," said Rick. "Like a dead body."

"Can't let that interfere with your personal plans. You're in the business of finding dead bodies."

Rick put his hand over Patty's. "Chuck's right. We need to make time to talk soon."

Patty smiled. "I'd like that."

Dinner was served and the conversation stopped while everyone began enjoying their dinner. Before they'd finished their entrees, Chuck's quiet laughter broke the silence. "Did I ever tell you about the Chief ME we had for a while? A guy named Joe with a dark sense of humor?"

"No," said Rick. "Must have been after I left, but I'm already wishing I had been there. Tell us about him."

Chuck couldn't help but smile as he reminisced. "Well, there was a murder case, and I took a rookie to the ME's exam room with me. About two minutes into it, the rookie fainted and hit his head on the floor. I appealed to the ME. 'Oh, my God,' I said as the blood pooled around the rookie's head. 'Do something.'

"The doc's response was 'He needs a doctor. Call 911.'

"I replied, somewhat shocked by that request, 'You are a doctor!'"

Patty and Rick were enjoying the story. "And his response?" asked Rick.

"He looked at me in all seriousness and said, 'Not that kind of doctor. I only work on dead people. Call 911.'"

"Oh my gosh," said Patty smiling, "Joe sounds like quite a character. Did you call 911?"

"I did, and the rookie was carried away on a stretcher."

Rick shook his head. "Any more humorous anecdotes of him you can share?"

Chuck set his beer down. "Yeah, there are several." He looked at Rick. "Do you remember Burkhard? Short, skinny guy. He wasn't SWAT, but he badly wanted to be. He must have approached me three or four times asking what was necessary for him to join us."

"You know," said Rick, "I do remember a guy who talked with me a couple of times about what was necessary to be a member of the SWAT team. Did he ever make it?"

"No. He left the department not long after you did. So I wasn't there to see this, but Joe shared something with me about Burkhard. It was Burkhard's first time standing across the metal table from Joe. One of the detectives brought him in. Burkhard was dressed in a white shirt and khaki pants."

Patty laughed. "I know where this is going."

"Yep," said Rick, smiling.

Chuck put up a hand to quiet them and let him go on. "Joe finished the autopsy, and before they left, he handed Burkhard a mirror." Chuck looked at the floor and laughed. "The rookie was momentarily confused and noticeably embarrassed by the fact that his white shirt was covered with small red spots. He blurted out, 'My shirt is ruined.' He then turned to the detective. 'Why didn't you warn me?'"

Rick laughed. "I imagine Joe was enjoying this immensely. What was the detective's response?"

"Joe enjoyed it every time it happened. The detective told Burkhard that we all learn by doing, and that the lesson that day was that where there are autopsies, there are also blood and flies."

"Great story," said Rick. "I wish I had known Joe. Sounds like the kind of ME that would make autopsies much easier to attend. I never got used to the sight or the smell."

Chuck downed the last part of his beer. "Yeah, Joe made both a lot more bearable."

Patty put her napkin on the table. "Ready to go?"

The three of them walked out.

Rick drove to Patty's house and walked her to the door. "I look forward to a day soon when I won't be leaving you on the doorstep."

"Let's make time to talk next weekend. We should be clear on what we each want."

"I'd like that, Patty."

Rick returned to the car and drove on to his place.

Walking up to the house, Chuck mentioned his plans. "I'll move out and into my condo next week. Once I'm in, I'll have you and Patty over."

"Sounds great, Chuck."

"And speaking of Patty: Don't let her go, Rick. She's a good person and is clearly in love with you."

Rick opened the front door. "I have no plans to let her go. She and I will do some serious talking this weekend."

CHAPTER 23

Patty put down her coffee cup and put her purse away. "Memorable stories from Chuck last night. I understand how you and he enjoyed working together."

Rick smiled. "Yeah, we relished the humor whenever possible. It provided much-needed small breaks in the day-to-day human tragedy that comes with the job."

"Crystal's here, in the interview room. She brought her attorney with her. We should go in when you're done with your pastry."

Rick swallowed. "I'm done." He crumpled up the white bag and threw a long shot toward the corner trash can.

Patty watched the paper wad drop into the can. "Let's hope our interview is as good as your basketball skills."

Rick smiled. "I'll see what I can do. Am I the bad guy, if needed?"

"Always."

The detectives entered the room and sat with their backs to the mirror, looking at Crystal and her attorney on the opposite side of the table. Crystal appeared composed, too much so for a woman suspected of murder.

Patty smiled. "Thank you for coming in, Crystal. We just have a few questions. Your answers may help us to find Grant's killer. Please give us your full name."

Crystal shrugged her shoulders. "I figure you know it, or you wouldn't have me in here."

Silence filled the room. "Okay, my name is Crystal Lynn Wellingham."

"Thank you. We're here, Crystal, to discuss the death of your husband, Grant Wellingham, and any role you played in his demise."

Crystal glanced at her attorney, looked back at Patty, and nodded. "Ask what you want. I had nothing to do with Grant's death."

"Good. How did you learn of your husband's death?"

Crystal wriggled in her chair, looked up at the ceiling, and then down at the tabletop. "As I recall, Detective, you told me." She looked up. "Don't you remember?"

Patty ignored the question. "Tell me how Grant died."

"Well, you told me that too. This seems a bit of a farce." Crystal appealed to her attorney. "Do I really need to tell the detectives what they already know?"

"You're under no obligation to tell them anything, Crystal."

Crystal looked quite sure of herself. "Oh, I don't mind." She faced Patty and began talking as though she were telling a children's story. "Grant was stabbed with something and cut up into pieces. He, or his body parts, were then put into a barrel, covered with lye, and rolled into the Ferry Creek reservoir."

Patty went quickly on to the next question. "Was he alive when cut up?"

Crystal hesitated. "Well, I'm sure he wasn't cut up alive. So, no. He was dead."

"So whatever he was stabbed with was strong enough to kill him first?"

"Yes."

"So you know what he was stabbed with?"

Crystal paused again. She opened her eyes a little wider and looked left and right a few times, as though thinking about the question. "He would not have been cut up alive."

Patty tilted her head as though puzzled. "How do you know that? How do you know that he wasn't tortured by having one limb at a time removed before dying?"

Crystal lost some of the poise she walked in with. "Because what you're describing would be inhuman. I'm sure Grant was killed first."

"What was used to stab him?"

The attorney quickly advised Crystal, "Don't answer that."

Crystal complied with her attorney's advice, so Patty circled back to the manner of death. "Do you know someone who has the ability to cut a man into pieces while he's still alive?"

"No, I don't, and I wish you'd quit suggesting that."

Patty softened her voice. "Oh, I'm sorry, Crystal, but I just want to make sure I'm clear on what you're telling us. How do you know Grant was killed before being dismembered?"

The attorney responded, "Don't answer that."

Patty glanced at Rick. He leaned forward. "Did Kevin Lacky help kill Grant?"

Crystal shook her head. "Kevin? Where did that come from?"

"We've already spoken with Kevin, Crystal. He was very helpful. We already know the answers to the questions we're asking. Kevin doesn't want to spend the rest of his life in prison. He's been talking to us. Are you willing to let him cut a deal while you do some serious time?"

Crystal furrowed her eyebrows and began to show anger. "What's that little rat been saying about me?"

"Only the truth, Crystal, and he's done a lot of talking. Not just about you but also about Blake."

At the mention of Blake's name Crystal's poised persona disappeared and she stiffened. "What do you know about Blake?"

"Enough to know that he's not taking a rap for you. You're all alone in this, Crystal. Was it Blake who killed Grant?"

Crystal looked at her attorney. "Can we talk alone?"

The attorney looked at Patty. "I need a few minutes to talk with my client."

"Sure. We'll step out. Just let the officer outside the door know when you're ready."

The detectives left the room and walked down the hall to their office.

Chuck was seated at Rick's desk, flipping his balisong. He stood up to move when Rick walked in.

Rick put up his hand. "No need to move. This won't be long. Crystal was taken aback when we mentioned Blake's name. She wants to consult her attorney."

"You think she's going to talk?" asked Chuck.

"Difficult to say. I don't expect her to give us anything substantial until we can tell her we've got Blake." Rick looked at Patty. "Your thoughts?"

"I agree, though we clearly got through to her that we know more than she thought we did."

An officer came to the door. "They're ready for you."

"Thanks," said Patty. She looked at Rick. "Let's find out what they have to say."

The detectives sat down, and Patty addressed Crystal. "You ready to tell us why you killed your husband or had him killed?"

Crystal had regained some confidence during the break. "You have no evidence that I had anything to do with Grant's murder. I don't care what Kevin told you. I'm not answering any more of your questions."

"Okay, Crystal. That's your right, but out of curiosity, how did you know that Grant was stabbed with something that killed him?"

Crystal looked at her attorney who made a motion for Crystal not to answer the question. Crystal ignored the attorney's advice. "Well, I guess Kevin must have told me."

Crystal's attorney shook her head, and Patty and Rick exchanged a quick glance.

Patty then addressed Crystal. "So how would Kevin know unless he was involved in the murder? You knew, and yet you did nothing to stop him? That suggests strongly that you wanted Grant dead and talked Blake and Kevin into doing your bidding."

Crystal's eyes narrowed and her soft facial expression hardened.

Her attorney stood up. "She's done answering questions, Detectives."

"No problem," said Patty. "We'll get the rest of the information we want from Kevin and Blake. They are both hoping to cut a deal."

After returning to her office, Patty shared with Chuck what was said in the interview.

Chuck listened to Patty. "You need to find Blake to wrap things up. The geofence efforts should produce results by later today. I'd like to see where Blake spends his time."

Rick picked up his keys. "Why don't we get something to eat? Maybe we'll have those results by the time we get back."

CHAPTER 24

Upon returning to the office after lunch, Patty checked her email. She'd received the geofence information and printed out the pages for Rick and Chuck to read.

Chuck was the first to interpret the information. "The number we assume belongs to Blake shows up several times in Crescent City."

Patty glanced at her file notes. "According to Blake's sister, that may be where his girlfriend lives."

Rick looked at a map. "That number also shows up in Josephine County about ten miles from Cave Junction. The area is outside of the city limits."

"Rick and I will go to Crescent City first," said Patty. "Learn what we can from the girlfriend."

They all agreed and, thirty minutes later, arrived at the girlfriend's apartment. Patty knocked on the front door. Rick stood behind her so as not to appear threatening.

Patty knocked a second time, and the door slowly opened. A small-statured woman in her twenties stood in a cotton dress and worn tennis shoes. She looked at Patty and Rick before quietly asking, "Yes?"

Patty smiled. "Are you Kelly?"

The young woman was hesitant. "Why do you want to know?"

Patty showed her badge. "I'm Detective Patty O'Toole. This is Detective Rick Starker. We're hoping you can answer a few questions for us."

The woman looked puzzled. "You want to ask me questions? What about?"

"We're looking for Blake Cirelli, and we've been told that you know him and may know where he is."

The woman paused before speaking and then started closing the door. "I don't know where he is."

Patty put her hand out. "Please, Kelly."

The woman hesitated with the door and stared at Patty. "How do you know my name?"

"Blake's sister gave your name to us. We need to ask Blake about an incident he may know something about. If he does, he could be very helpful. Do you know where we might find him?"

"You say he can be helpful to the police?"

"That's right, Kelly. He may have information that will help us to solve a case."

"Well, okay. I guess you can come in but only to ask a few questions. I have to be at the church in an hour."

Patty and Rick followed Kelly into the apartment. "Let's sit at the kitchen table. Can I get you some water?"

"No, thank you," said Patty. The detectives took a seat, and Rick took his pen and tablet from his pocket.

Patty used a friendly approach with her questions. "Have you known Blake very long?"

"No, only about six months. We met when he started mowing the lawn at my church."

"Does he live here with you?"

The young woman smiled. "Yes, Blake's my boyfriend. It's only been six months, but we hit it off right away. You know what I mean? Sometimes love is like that."

"I understand. What does Blake do for a living?"

Kelly thought for a moment. "Well, he does the yard work for our church and some of the parishioners. Everybody loves him because he's so polite. That's not something you find nowadays. You know what I mean?"

Patty glanced at Rick and then answered, "I think I do, Kelly. Does Blake have a place of his own? A house or apartment? Someplace he stays when he's not here with you?"

Kelly's eyebrows lowered as she gave the question some thought. "That's an interesting question. I guess I've never asked him. He said he was living in an apartment when he and I first met, and that he gave that up when he moved in with me. I'm sure that he would have told me if he had a house."

Rick stood up. "May I use your bathroom?"

Kelly pointed. "Well, sure. It's down the hall."

While Rick was gone, Patty continued her questions. "Has Rick ever mentioned anyone by the name of Crystal or Kevin?"

Kelly shook her head. "No, I don't remember those names. I don't think they go to my church. Are they part of the case you think Blake can help you with?"

"Yes, Kelly, they are." Before Patty went on, a car door closed out front.

Kelly stood up. "That's probably him now. I'll let him know you need his help."

As Kelly left to greet Blake, Rick walked back into the room. He looked at Patty and shook his head. "Nothing. Not even an aspirin."

Patty lowered her voice, hearing footsteps coming up the front porch. "Blake is here. Let's not take him in right now. I'd rather ask questions and get as much information as we can. He has to have a place other than here with Kelly or with his sister."

The front door opened, and Kelly walked into the room with her boyfriend. "This is Blake. I told him you need his help."

Blake stared at Patty and Rick. "Why are you here at Kelly's place?"

Patty stepped forward. "We were looking for you, Blake."

"Who told you to look for me here?"

"No one specific. But since you're here, we'd like to ask a few questions."

Blake stood with his arms crossed over his chest. "What if I don't want to answer your questions?"

Kelly looked surprised. "Blake, this doesn't sound like you. Let's do what we can to help the police do their job. It's just a few questions."

Blake looked at Kelly and then back at Patty. "What is it you want to know?"

Patty smiled. "Thank you, Blake. Can you tell us where you stay when you're not here at Kelly's?"

"Kelly said you needed my help. What difference does it make where I stay?"

"It helps us to establish your credibility, Blake, knowing whether you have a house of your own."

Kelly's facial expression was one of interest in Blake's answer.

Blake looked at Kelly before answering. "No, I don't."

"Okay. Can you tell us your relationship to Crystal and Kevin?"

Blake's demeanor changed as he became angry. "I don't know those people, and I don't know how this can help with whatever case you're working on. I've got work to do, so you need to leave now."

Patty looked at Rick. "Well, that's a surprise." She turned back to Blake. "I find your answer curious because Crystal and Kevin know you. Maybe you just need a little more time. Are you sure you don't know either of them?"

"I meet a lot of people, so it's possible I mowed their lawn. Now I'm asking that you leave."

Patty nodded. "We have more questions. If you don't have time to answer them now, you can stop by the police station this afternoon and we'll finish up then."

Blake noticed Kelly smiling at him. "Sure, if I get the time, I'll stop by."

"That will be very helpful, Blake."

Patty walked to the car and looked back. "He's hiding something,"

Rick pulled out. "He is, and he doesn't want Kelly to know about it. I'm guessing he'll leave soon and head out to his secret location. Want to tail him?"

"Yes, but we won't approach him or his place until we have backup."

Rick pulled over on a side street, and they waited. Ten minutes later, they watched Blake cross in front of them. Rick slowly pulled around the corner and followed at a safe distance.

Patty called Chuck and let him know what they were doing. "Can you tell me where in Cave Junction Blake's number showed up?"

"Give me a minute and I'll call you back. Do you want company?"

"Not sure yet. If we locate the place, I'll text you the address."

"I'll be ready."

Blake drove out of Crescent City and onto Highway 199 toward Cave Junction. The detectives followed. Twenty minutes later, while they were driving through Gasquet, Chuck called Patty.

"I've got the coordinates for you. The phone was used west of downtown in Cave Junction. I'll send you a photo of the map. Looks like a lot of it may be dirt roads. Be careful tracking him. If he thinks you're onto the location, he may rabbit on you."

"We'll follow for as long as we can without being too conspicuous." Patty disconnected the call and looked at the map Chuck emailed to her. "It appears that his place is on the outskirts of Cave Junction. It's going to be difficult keeping far enough away. I've got binoculars in the trunk. If we get to where you can stop without losing him, I'll jump out and get them."

Two cars drove past Rick in the passing lane and merged between Blake and Rick. "They must be going to a fire. Looks like they're slowing down up here to turn into that RV park."

Rick sped up once the cars had turned. "Darn, I don't see him."

"I don't either, "said Patty. "So he's disappeared into thin air, or he turned off someplace between here and the RV park we passed. Turn around when you can."

Rick did a U-turn and started back.

Patty pointed. "Up there. See the mailboxes?"

"I see them. This might be a good time for you to call for backup. Ask Chuck to come out too. I'll keep going until we know which parcel is his."

Patty attempted to call Chuck on her cell without luck. "There's no cell service here, Rick. We need to drive back out to the highway and possibly down to the RV park we passed. I'll make the call, and we can return here. I'm also going to call the LT and see if he can help expedite a telephonic search warrant for us."

"No problem. I'll drive a little further to find a place wide enough to turn around."

"Stop," said Patty. "It's Blake's car. There, in the clearing." She retrieved the binoculars from the trunk. "I see his car and a house. That's it, Rick."

Rick found a clearing wide enough to turn the car around. He drove back to the highway where Patty's phone registered service. She tried calling Chuck, heard the phone ring, and motioned to Rick that the call was going through. When Chuck answered, Patty spoke quickly. "We need backup, Chuck. Let Brad and Pete know we want them here too. We've followed Blake to a parcel of land off the highway. Take the first driveway on your right after passing the Restful Tree RV Park. There are three mailboxes. It will take you about an hour and fifteen minutes to get here. Rick and I will sit on the road near the access to Blake's property. We'll wait for backup before going in."

"Leaving now," said Chuck.

Patty called the lieutenant. "Hello, LT. Rick and I have found our suspect at the property where we believe he committed the Barrel Bones murder. We need to get inside the house, any other dwellings on the property, and his car, as well as confiscate his cell phone and computer. Can you help us out by obtaining a telephonic search warrant?"

"I can do that, Detective. You and Rick are not to approach the suspect without backup. Understood?"

"Understood. Brad, Pete, and Chuck are on their way."

"Good. I'll take care of the warrant and text it to Brad. There's a chance he will still be on the highway and able to receive text messages."

"Thank you, LT."

Rick slowly drove along the dirt road surrounded by heavy forest. Patty noticed how blocked they were by trees. "Let's hope no one comes at us from the opposite direction. This road is hardly wide enough for one car, much less two."

"Judging from what we've seen, I doubt there will be much traffic. And, if need be, I'll hug the side of the road."

Rick drove slowly, approaching the entrance to the property where Blake had turned in.

Patty picked up the binoculars. "He must be inside. No sign of anyone else."

Rick began pulling forward. "The turnaround we used should be just up ahead. Then we can drive back to the entrance to his driveway and wait for the others."

* * *

Upon arriving, Blake hurried into his house and called Crystal.

"What's up, Blake?"

"We've got a problem, Crystal."

"I know, Blake. Kevin's in jail, I'm having a hard time running my business with this burner phone since the cops have not yet returned the phone they took, and then there's you thinking this is all my fault."

"We have a bigger problem than that, Crystal. Those two detectives showed up at Kelly's apartment."

"Your girlfriend's apartment? What did they want from her?"

"They wanted to know where I was. They also asked her if I had a place of my own."

"Well, Blake, that sounds like they really don't know anything. They're still just guessing. What's the urgency?"

"I showed up while they were there. They questioned me about you and Kevin."

"What did you say?"

"I told them I didn't know you. That you could be one of the parishioners. But I know they didn't believe me."

"Where are you now, Blake?"

"I'm at my place. I left Kelly's and drove here. I need time to think."

"Listen, Blake. This is no different than before. If we all keep our mouths shut, we'll be okay."

"Yeah? What about your friend Kevin? I know he won't keep his mouth shut. This is your fault, Crystal. You should never have let him in on our business."

"Don't go blaming everything on me, Blake. You were the one who hired the guy who couldn't manage the job. Where did you find him? One of your drug customers? He was supposed to eliminate our problem, and all he did was create a bigger one.”

“I've spoken to him, and he'll finish the job.”

“Look, Blake, I don't know that there's anything else we can do. My attorney said that the police haven't arrested me because they've got nothing concrete to charge me with.”

“Your attorney? I told you not to talk to any attorney.”

“It's not a problem. I wasn't going to be questioned by the police without my attorney present. I haven't told them anything. Just lay low until things quiet down. Then we'll decide what to do.”

“Yeah, okay.”

CHAPTER 25

Chuck had already arrived when Brad and Pete showed up. They all drove past the entrance to Blake's and met up with Patty and Rick. Patty walked over to Brad. "Got it?"

"Right here," said Brad, showing the search warrant on his phone. "The LT sent this to me about twenty minutes ago."

Patty smiled. "That was fast!" She then addressed the group. "This is the plan. Rick and I will go to the door. Brad and Pete go behind the house in case he takes off out the back door. Chuck will remain out front and watch our backs." Patty looked at Chuck. "What do you expect he'll do?"

"He'll run out the back door." He looked at Brad and Pete. "I'd place myself as close as I could to the back door without being so close that he could hit me coming out. We've got the element of surprise. That counts for a lot in this kind of situation. We'd like to take him back alive, but don't hesitate to protect yourselves." Brad and Pete nodded their agreement.

Patty spoke with Rick. "Let's bring the cars up to just before his driveway and then walk in. There's no fence, so I don't expect a dog in the yard."

Rick let the others know where to line up their cars. He directed them to drive up the road about two hundred feet where they could pull over and make a U-turn. Once all cars had turned around, they all slowly drove forward, blocking the driveway. They each walked to their assigned positions.

Rick and Patty quietly climbed the stairs to the porch. They could hear the TV on inside. Patty knocked and kept her eyes on the front window. Rick put his shield up at the peephole.

Within ten seconds, they heard Pete at the back of the house. "We've got him."

The cuffed suspect was brought around to the front of the house. Then Pete left to get the car.

Blake tried to shake off Brad's hold of him. "What is this? You have no right to arrest me. And you have no right to be on my property."

"You're wrong, Blake," said Patty. "We've got a search warrant for this property. Want to save us a little time and let us know what we'll find?"

Blake quit struggling with Brad. "You won't find nothing. So what's this about?"

"I told you at Kelly's place," said Patty. "We had a few more questions."

Patty, Rick, and Chuck entered the house. Rick began searching bedrooms while Patty went into the kitchen. Chuck sat down in Blake's living room chair, pulled out the balisong from his back pocket, and began fluttering it.

"All clear," hollered Rick after searching both bedrooms.

In the kitchen, Patty looked through cupboards. She opened the refrigerator which, except for a case of beer and a few waters, was empty. Next, she pulled down the oven door. "In here, Rick."

Rick walked into the kitchen and looked at the oven. Inside was a large plastic bag filled with white powder. "It doesn't connect him with the murder, but it is a reason to arrest him while we continue to search. Let's take a look in his car."

The detectives walked through the living room toward the front when Chuck stopped them. He pointed to a table where a small amount of white powder had been spilled. "I assumed at first that the powder was meth, but now I'm thinking it's lye. And since there's no evidence in this house of a lye solution having been prepared, I'm guessing there must be a building of some sort out back, probably beyond the tree line, keeping it out of sight."

"Let's check," said Patty. "I'll have Brad arrest Blake, and then I'll catch up with you both."

Brad was standing next to his car when Patty approached. "We're going to search the forest area behind the house. We found a large quantity of what appears to be meth, so we've got him on possession for sale. Arrest him and hold him in the car."

When Patty caught up with Rick and Chuck, they were just beyond the first line of trees behind the house.

Rick saw Patty approaching. "This has to be it. I'm guessing he made it himself. I've seen a lot of greenhouses made with corrugated plastic siding like this. The difference is that he's painted this black to keep anyone from seeing what's inside."

"Do you have something to break the lock with?"

"No need. The lock's screwed onto the plastic and will be easy to pry off. I guess he didn't expect anything other than animals back here." Rick opened the door to the shed. He and Patty stepped inside. The large plastic jugs of water and boxes of lye on a shelf gave them what they needed.

"We've got him," said Patty. "I'll call forensics and get them up here. You let Brad and Pete know what we've found. I want to talk to Blake before they take him back to Gold Beach."

Blake was in the back seat of Brad's police vehicle. Patty opened the door. "We've got you, Blake."

"Yeah? For a small amount of meth. I'll be out in no time."

"I don't think so, Blake. We found your little work shed out back. Forensics are on their way up here now. We'll find enough evidence to put you away for both murders. You won't see the outside again."

Blake brought his hands up in front of him, palms facing Patty. "Wait a minute. What do you mean by both murders? You can't pin that mushroom woman on me."

Patty stared at Blake. "Mushroom woman?"

Blake shook his head. "No. No. No. I know what you're doing. And I know Kevin's already mentioned my name. But I had nothing to do with killing his wife."

Patty closed the door and began walking away. Brad started the car when Blake yelled at him to stop. "I want to talk to the detective."

Brad waited while Patty walked back to the car and opened the door. "What?"

Blake leaned his head toward Patty. "I know what you want, but I'm not saying anything without a deal. I don't want to spend my life in prison."

"We'll see you in the jail, Blake. Right after we talk with Crystal." Patty instructed Brad to go ahead.

The detectives and Chuck waited for forensics to arrive. Rick mimicked fluttering a balisong for Chuck. "Your knife fluttering worked again."

Chuck shrugged. "It helps."

Once Brad and Pete left with Blake, Patty pulled out her cell phone, called, and got through to her lieutenant.

"O'Toole? Success?"

"Very much so. We found enough meth to get him on that alone, but we've also found the building in which he stored his lye and evidence that he used it. Forensics are on their way."

"That's good, O'Toole. Any visible sign of having cut up the victim?"

"Not in the shack, sir. It's only about ten by fifteen. Not enough room. But there are a couple of makeshift benches outside. I'm hoping forensics finds blood there."

"Where is the suspect now?"

"Brad and Pete are taking him in. Before he left, he confirmed Bella Lacky was murdered, though he maintains his innocence in the act."

"You and Rick have made great progress on this, O'Toole. Good work."

"Not just Rick and me, LT. Chuck is the one who spotted what he believed to be lye in the living room. He then suggested there had to be another building and that we should search the woods."

"Well, please extend my thanks to Chuck too. I'll talk with the three of you when you are all here together."

"Thanks, LT. And thanks again for your help with the telephonic warrant. Your contacting the judge made a huge difference in timing."

"Happy to be of assistance, Detective. Now, get the proof you need to solve both cases."

"That's our plan, LT. I'll let you know when we do."

Patty returned to find Chuck showing Rick how to flutter his knife. "The LT is impressed with the work all three of us completed here today. He said he'll be talking with us. He also suggested we get both cases solved."

Rick handed Chuck his knife and then turned to Patty. "Did you tell him that we appreciated his help with the telephonic search warrant?"

"I did. He said what he always does: 'Happy to help.'" Patty paused as two cars turned down the driveway and came up to the house.

The forensic experts stepped out of their cars already gowned in disposable body suits. The team leader, Hank, spoke with Patty. "What have we got?"

"There's powdered meth on a table in the living room and a large bag of it in the oven. We'll take the bag with us after you've had a chance to go through the house. In back of the house and just beyond the line of trees is a small shack. It appears as though he stored his lye and water in the shed along with gardening tools and supplies. There are also two wooden table-like structures which may be where he dissected his victim."

Hank gave the information to the other two members of his team, then directed his attention to Patty. "Thanks for the specifics. We'll fully suit up since we don't know what we're dealing with."

"One other thing," Patty said. "The victim was stabbed with some sort of sharp item. We need to see anything you find with blood and/or human tissue on it."

"We'll be thorough, Detective."

Patty watched the three workers put on their masks and respirators, chemical spill boots, and gloves. They taped each other's gloves as an extra precaution.

When forensics finished in the house, Rick removed the bag of meth, put it in an evidence bag, and set it in the back of his trunk. He left a receipt on the table and photographed it as proof.

Patty let Hank know that they were leaving. "Let me know as soon as you find anything that might prove our victim was killed here."

"Will do, Detective."

An hour into their drive back to the coast, Patty's phone vibrated. She looked at Rick. "It's forensics." She answered, "O'Toole."

"We can confirm, Detective, that we've found both blood and tissue on the tables outside of the shack. There is lye powder in the house. In addition to the lye you saw in the shack, there's a dried lye solution on the ground. It appears as though he built a tripod structure to use as a pot hanger to boil something over a fire. Also in the area of dried lye on the ground is a circular indentation. We'll run tests, but it suggests the outline of a barrel. We also found odds and ends such as green, lima, and castor bean seeds, flowerpots, and gardening tools, all with Blake's prints on them. At the lab we'll be able to quickly confirm whether the blood and tissue are human. It will take a little longer to determine whether it's a match to the DNA on your victim's toothbrush."

"Anything resembling a murder weapon?"

"No, but you may want to search a wider perimeter around the shack. There're also some areas of dirt that look recently turned."

Patty gave Rick a thumbs-up as she responded, "Thank you."

After ending the call, Patty gave the forensic results to Rick and Chuck. "There was no weapon found, but there are several areas of recently upturned dirt we should check out. I'll talk with the LT, but there's no question that we now have the key suspect in the Barrel Bones murder. We can hold Blake for the meth. We need to decide on timing for admonishing him and questioning him about the murder."

"Let's go over what we know," said Rick, "based upon information each suspect has given us."

"Good idea," said Patty. "To narrow down the clues, let's start with just the murder of Grant Wellingham. I'll start. Kevin was the first one of the three to mention Blake's involvement. Kevin said it was primarily Blake and Crystal involved in the murder. Crystal recognized Blake's name but didn't say any more about him."

Rick mentioned the crime scene. "We now are waiting on confirmation that Blake killed Wellingham, dismembered the body, and created the lye solution."

"What we need now," said Patty, "is for Blake or Crystal to fold and incriminate Kevin as Blake's accomplice." She set down her pen. "Let's interview

Crystal when we get back. See if she'll want to give up Blake once we tell her what we've got. Chuck, do you have any ideas?"

"Not much more than you two have stated. Crystal has been pretty slippery. She's clearly the smartest of the three and has done her best to leave no evidence. I don't think Blake will say anything unless he wants to talk about getting life rather than the death penalty. Kevin is afraid of Blake and Crystal, but he's more afraid of going to prison. That being said, Crystal's business is her life. She killed her husband and gave up her kids for it. So who will give up the others first? I think they'll all turn on each other."

"I'll go along with that," said Rick.

Patty agreed. "Me too. We'll let Blake sit and worry while we discuss the best way to approach him."

CHAPTER 26

"We've got to find something that clearly ties Crystal to the murder. With the right approach, Blake may talk. Your thoughts, Chuck?"

"Blake knows he's going to spend the rest of his life in prison no matter what he gives you. I'd impress upon him that unless he can prove she was involved, she'll go back to her business and forget all about him."

Patty nodded. "I like that approach."

She looked at Rick and he agreed. "Let's try it."

The detectives sat across the table from Blake and his attorney. Blake's eyes met Patty's. The demeanor he'd shown previously was gone. His eyes were now cold and dark as she explained his predicament.

"We've got you for the meth, Blake. You'll go to prison for that. And we've received confirmation that lye, blood, and tissue were found at the shack behind your house. We have no doubt your fingerprints will be all over everything. If the blood and tissue are those of Grant Wellingham, there's a chance you'll be sentenced to death or, at the least, spend the rest of your life in prison."

Blake sneered and remained silent while Patty explained. "We've spoken with Crystal. She let us know that if anyone was going to get a deal, it better be her. And from the way she tells it, she'll soon be back in her luxurious office."

Blake momentarily looked concerned. "You're lying. No way can she get out of this."

Patty raised her eyebrows as if surprised. "There's not much we can hold her on since she had nothing to do with the murders. She told us that it was all you and Kevin."

Blake's otherwise calm demeanor was cracking, and his eyes narrowed. "She said that? That it was me and Kevin?"

"She did, Blake. Is she not telling the truth?"

Blake laughed as he got the words out. "Grant was her husband. He wouldn't be dead if she hadn't requested and paid for it."

Rick leaned forward. "Paid for it?"

Blake's attorney interrupted Blake. "Don't answer that."

"Why? They're going to find my fingerprints in the shack. And they're going to find that the blood is Grant's. There may be nothing I can do to lessen my sentence, but there's no way I'm letting Crystal walk away from this."

The attorney insisted again, "Don't say anything else."

Blake looked around the room and at his handcuffed hands. "Crystal knows everything about the murders. She recruited Kevin to stack Grant's body parts into the barrel and help me load and unload it into the water at Ferry Creek Dam."

Patty quietly responded, "That's information that, if proven, could definitely alter Crystal's future. Do you have proof? Emails or a copy of the check she paid you with?"

Blake shook his head. "No. She paid me in cash."

"No problem," said Patty. "The deposit will show up on your bank statement."

"You found my meth. So it shouldn't surprise you that I don't use a bank. I keep my cash hidden."

Patty sighed in disappointment. "Well, Blake, that doesn't bode well for putting Crystal away. Are you sure the two of you didn't communicate at all using email?"

"No. That was Crystal's first rule. The only emails or texts were to set up a phone call. All planning was done over the phone."

Patty looked at Rick and shrugged. "Well, Blake, it seems Crystal will be the only one to avoid prison."

Blake leaned into the table. "Ask Kevin. He'll tell you she was involved all the way with both murders."

"We've spoken to Kevin. The problem is that neither of you have any proof."

"We're done talking," said Patty as she and Rick left the room. They met up again with Chuck in the hall. Patty smiled. "Your idea worked. And we can now arrest Kevin again, this time for the murder of Wellingham."

Chuck nodded in agreement. "Now all you need is proof that Crystal and Kevin were involved in both murders."

Rick yawned. "Let's talk again with Kevin tomorrow. We'll tell him that Blake won't get out. Maybe that will free up his ability to tell us more and offer evidence."

* * *

"You're in early this morning." Patty set a bakery bag down on Rick's desk.

Rick opened the bag and smiled. "Exactly what my brain needs to go with the coffee refill I'm about to get. I woke up early thinking about the Barrel Bones case and figured I would think better sitting at my desk with the file."

Patty picked up Rick's coffee mug. "I want to hear your thoughts, but first let me get us some fuel."

Patty returned to the office and set Rick's coffee on his desk. She took a doughnut out of the bag and sat down. "Any specific part of the case that caused you to wake up early?"

"There is. Yesterday, Blake said that Kevin stabbed Wellingham. We need to find that weapon. I think Brad and Pete should go back to Blake's house and search the grounds. I also think they need to dig in back of the house."

Patty swallowed her coffee. "I agree. I'll let Brad know that he can take a third officer if he thinks it necessary." She picked up her phone. "Maybe I can catch him before he comes into the office."

Brad was up when his cell phone rattled. "Hey, Patty."

"Good morning, Brad. Would it be possible for you and Pete to go back to Blake's house this morning?"

"Sure. We searching for something specific?"

"The murder weapon used to stab Wellingham. Something along the lines of an icepick but not necessarily as narrow. Search the house first, then the area around the makeshift shack and benches."

"How far a perimeter do you want us to search?"

"From the house to about fifteen feet behind the shack. Take a shovel. If you find anything at all other than dirt, give me a call. We'll send a team to help out."

"Okay. Pete and I will head out there now."

"Keep me informed, Brad."

"Will do, Detective."

Patty's cell phone illuminated. She looked at caller ID. "It's forensics. Detective O'Toole."

"Detective, this is Alex over at the lab."

"Good morning, Alex. I have you on speaker phone. What can you tell us?"

"We've been able to positively match the DNA from Grant's toothbrush to the blood and tissue found on and around the workbenches."

"That's very helpful, Alex. Thank you. Hope your day goes well."

"You're welcome, Detective. There's one more thing before you go. We found blood other than Wellingham's. No way to know who it belongs to."

"Another victim? That's troubling but not altogether unexpected. Thanks again."

"Sure, Detective. I hope you find who it belongs to."

"So do we, Alex."

Rick and Chuck waited for Patty to end the call. She looked up from her desk.

"This assures us that Blake will be convicted, but we still need proof that one of them stabbed Wellingham before dismembering him."

The atmosphere in the room was pensive. Rick got up and walked over to the window. He took a moment to appreciate the rainbow of colors created by the sun's reflection in the lawn sprinklers. "Another victim. Blake's been busier than we thought."

Patty flipped back a few pages in her file. "Kevin mentioned a first murder, meaning before Wellingham."

Chuck sat against the wall enjoying his coffee. "That means all three of them were involved with and knew each other before the murders of Wellingham and Lacky."

Rick turned around. "We need to bring this up in our interview with Kevin."

Patty removed her jacket from the back of her chair. "The interview is scheduled for nine-thirty. Let's leave now and give ourselves room for roadwork delays."

At the jail, Chuck watched the interview again from outside the window in an adjoining room. Patty and Rick sat down with Kevin and his attorney.

Patty's greeting was cordial. "Good morning, Kevin. Are you enjoying your stay?"

Kevin looked tired and disheveled. "I'm not going to answer that. I am putting up with this because I fully expect to be set free soon."

"I don't think that's going to happen, Kevin. Not with what we now know."

"What do you mean by that?"

Patty leaned back in her chair. "Well, for starters, Blake's been honest with us. He's let us know that you were very much involved with the murders of both Grant Wellingham and Bella Lacky."

Kevin's knee started jumping, and he gritted his teeth. "He's just angry because you have proof on him, and you can't prove anything he says about me."

Patty slowly shook her head. "Wrong again, Kevin. I think his testimony against you, when supported by Crystal, will be enough. And then there's your long wait to call 911 when your wife was dying. And let's not forget your participation in the first murder."

"I told you. I was only doing what Crystal and Blake made me do."

"I don't mean the murder of Wellingham, Kevin. I mean the first murder. The one before that."

Sweat beads formed on Kevin's forehead. "What? What first murder?"

Kevin's attorney looked sharply at her client and then quickly asked him not to speak.

Patty noticed her reaction. "You didn't know about the third murder, or first, if we count them chronologically, did you?"

The attorney addressed Kevin. "Don't answer any more questions, Kevin. We need to talk."

Kevin folded his arms on the table and laid his head face down on them. "This is turning into a big mess. Blake assured me and Crystal that we would never be suspected in the deaths. We just had to trust him. I don't know what to do now. Can I call Crystal?"

Patty softened her voice. "I'm sorry, Kevin. But, no, you can't call Crystal. Crystal is looking out for herself. She told us that you and Blake committed the murders. If that isn't true, you need to tell us what is."

Kevin lifted his head from his hands. "I can't. Blake has already tried to kill me. He'll make sure it happens if I tell you the truth. I just want to leave all of this and be alone. I want to go away to someplace far from here." Kevin looked into Patty's eyes. "Can you do that? Can the police take me someplace like in the witness protection plan?"

"I don't know, Kevin. I can tell that you are hurting. Tell me, how do you feel about Bella's death?"

Kevin jerked back his head as if accosted. "Bella? How do I feel about Bella's death? How can you even think of her when I'm in such pain? She was a witch. She was sleeping with her boss and used me. I'm glad she's dead."

Patty stayed with her calm, quiet questioning. "But she died such a horrific death. Suffering for hours there on your bathroom floor. I'm sure that must be the cause of a lot of your anguish."

Kevin scoffed. "My anguish? The cause of my anguish is the mess I'm in. The mess Blake and Crystal have put me in. I don't want to lose my condo and my job. Bella died a slow death because Crystal told me to delay calling 911 until Blake saw Bella. Then Blake came over and told me to wait fifteen minutes before making the call. He wanted time to get away. It wasn't a wish on my part to make Bella suffer like that. It was just timing. She just had to wait until Blake said I could call for help. Timing. That's all."

Kevin's attorney sat back in the chair and looked at Patty and Rick. "Enough?"

Patty held up her index finger asking for one more minute. "Kevin, who was the first person murdered?"

Kevin looked at Patty. "The first person?"

"Yes, you helped Crystal and Blake with a murder before Grant Wellingham."

"Oh, you mean Penny Rich. Crystal just asked if I'd help Blake move some body parts out of his car. That was just something I had to do for Crystal. I did it because she was helping me get situated in my business and paid me for it."

"Where did the body come from?"

Kevin's eyes became droopy. "I'm so tired." He looked at his attorney. "I need to lay down."

Kevin's attorney stood up. "That's enough for now."

"For now," said Patty. "We still have questions. We'll be back tomorrow."

The detectives left and joined Chuck in the adjoining room.

"Let's head back to the office," said Patty.

During the drive back, Patty's phone vibrated. "It's Blake's girlfriend." She tapped the phone. "Detective O'Toole."

"Hello, Detective, this is Kelly, Blake's girlfriend. You and the other detective came to my apartment."

"I remember," said Patty. "What can I do for you?"

"Well, this is kind of difficult. I don't know if Blake would want me telling you this, but it scares me, so I want to get rid of it."

"Get rid of what?"

"Well, it's a knife. Blake brought it over two or three weeks ago, wrapped in a towel. He put it under some clothes on a shelf in my closet. I didn't think about it again until yesterday when I learned Blake's in jail. I'm feeling very confused about him, and I don't want this knife in my apartment."

"Okay. We'll be over soon to pick it up. Please don't tell anyone else you have it."

"I won't. Thank you."

Patty looked at Rick. "Could be our murder weapon. Let's find out."

Thirty minutes later they arrived at Kelly's apartment. She opened the door holding the towel in her hands. Patty took it from her and carefully folded open the top of the towel.

"It's a stiletto," said Rick. "It fits the doc's description."

"Used for what?" asked Kelly.

"I'm sorry to have to tell you," said Patty, "but Blake's been arrested for murder."

Kelly's eyes opened wide. "Oh, no. That's horrible. Everyone at the church will be so sad about this. I don't know how I'll tell our pastor. I feel like such a fool."

"Don't be too hard on yourself. Blake is a manipulator who has tricked a lot of people into thinking he's an honest man. I've known others who used the church to shield their real character. Is there someone you can talk to?"

Kelly wiped the tears off her face. "Yes. I'll be okay. I just need to sit down." The door slowly closed as the detectives walked to their car.

After returning to Brookings, Rick sent the knife to the lab. "I expect this to provide proof that Blake murdered Wellingham. We have Kevin's confession, but without evidence that Crystal was involved, her case will depend on hearsay."

"There's still a chance," said Patty, "that we'll learn she's responsible for their first victim. I'll let the LT know what we've got."

Patty walked down the hall to find the lieutenant at his desk.

"Come in, O'Toole."

"Hi, LT. Do you have a minute?"

"I do. This about the Barrel Bones case?"

Patty sat down. "It is. We've just received the weapon we believe was used to kill Wellingham. A stiletto knife. Rick sent it to the lab."

"Where was it found?"

"Blake's girlfriend called us. He had hidden it in her apartment."

"That's a great find, O'Toole. This about wraps up everything."

"Yes, just about. We now have the murder weapon and can tie it to Blake for Wellingham's death. We've got Kevin for waiting until his wife had died before calling 911 and participating in disposal of Wellingham's body. According to both Blake and Kevin, Crystal is guilty of helping with both deaths, though we can't tie her directly to either. And then we have the third murder. Kevin admitted to being involved along with Crystal and Blake."

"Any idea what happened to the victim's body?"

"Well, Rick and I have discussed that. We're wondering if the hand we found in the sand about a year ago belongs to the victim."

"I know that cold case bothers you and Rick. It would be good to solve it."

"It would, LT. I'll let you know when we do."

The lieutenant nodded.

Patty got up and returned to the office where Rick was working on a report. "Where's Chuck this morning?"

"He texted me earlier. He's closing escrow and picking up the keys for his condo. Then he'll work on changing the utilities over and think about what he needs to furnish his place."

"He's got to be pretty excited."

"He is. He'll talk with us later this evening. I think he's leaving tomorrow and driving back to Boston to pick up a few things. I've been thinking that, since he'll be gone this weekend, you could come over, and we'll have that talk we've been planning."

"That would be great, Rick. I need to schedule Crystal's appointment for Monday before calling it a day. I've also got a couple of things to take care of at home this evening. I'll plan on joining you at your place about ten tomorrow if that works for you."

"That works. It will give me time to clean up a little before you arrive."

CHAPTER 27

Patty had begun packing when her mother called. "Hi, Mom. How was your trip?"

"I was just reflecting on that, Patty. The trip was great! Do you have time to hear about it now?"

"Sure, I have a little time. Tell me about it."

"Well, on my first day I drove up to Florence and stayed at a hotel on the Siuslaw River."

"Before you go on, Mom, can you tell me how the locals pronounce the name of the river?"

Maggie laughed. "Funny you should ask. I asked several people hearing several different pronunciations. Most of the responders broke the name into three syllables. They pronounced the name with a long letter i, as in the word sigh. The second syllable is u, and the third is slaw."

Patty slowly pronounced what her mother had instructed. "Sigh-u-slaw."

"That was the most common pronunciation."

"Did you have time to go into any of the shops?"

"I did. It was a very nice stroll down the street to the restaurant, where I ate a good serving of fish and chips. The next morning, I ate breakfast in a little restaurant on the highway before continuing my travels to the Mount Hood area."

"I'm not familiar with that part of the state, Mom. Where did you stay?"

"The property has a main restaurant building, an inn, and several small cabins. I had a room at the inn. The room was comfortable, the employees very nice, and my dinner choice was great. I had hoped to eat my dinner in the large dining area pictured on their website because it appears to be a comfortable room with a cozy fireplace."

"I take it you didn't get to eat there."

"There was a private party using the entire dining room, so I was asked to eat in the lounge. There were no other guests eating in the lounge at that time, so I think this is probably the slow season. And, at about 4,300 feet elevation with lots of hiking trails, it's really more of a destination for outdoor winter and hiking activities. I was on an adventure, however, so I'm glad I spent a night there and learned more about the area."

"As I recall, your next stop was Condon, where your friend lives. How was your visit?"

"My visit to Condon was great for many reasons. It was wonderful to see my friend again. Leanne and her husband were great hosts. The town of Condon is rich in history and has a museum and several small buildings filled with items of historical significance. There is an historic downtown area with several beautifully restored buildings. And you won't find any of them vacant or poorly maintained. There is a rule in Condon that you must either rent out your vacant property or sell it. Leanne and her husband are both very active in maintaining the beauty of the town and the integrity of its history.

"The museum area is made up of one large building and several smaller individual buildings. I went into a small one-bedroom residence that was fully furnished with everything you'd need back then. It even had a female manikin dressed like the lady of the house. The one-room schoolhouse is furnished with period items and a manikin teacher. A set of typed rules attached to one wall helped visitors understand what life was like back then for a teacher. The rules were for the female teacher and included her inability to court or marry."

"What was the punishment if she married?"

"She would lose her job."

"Wow! I guess that's why so many old western movies portray female teachers as single. Where did you stay?"

"I stayed at the Hotel Condon. It is an historic hotel that has been beautifully renovated. I found it to be very comfortable, and the employees were all quite pleasant."

"It seems that Condon was the highlight of your trip, Mom."

"Oh, yes, it was. Leanne and her husband have quite a lot of family in the area, several of whom I met. Their granddaughter and two nieces showed animals at the 4H auction we attended. That was fun. I had a wonderful time."

"I'm so happy for you, Mom, that your trip was such a success. I've enjoyed hearing about your adventures, and I know there's more. Can we get together soon for lunch?"

"We can do that, Patty. Before I go, how is Rick doing?"

"He's great. I'm going to his place tomorrow morning for the weekend. We are going to have a serious conversation."

"You mean the serious conversation you two have attempted many times over the past three years?"

"That's the one. But I don't think there's anything at work to interfere with it this time. We are going to make it happen, Mom."

"Nothing would make me happier, Patty."

"Thanks, Mom. I know you are fond of Rick. I'll call after work today, and we can decide on a lunch date."

"I look forward to both subjects. Now, get back to your packing and enjoy your weekend."

"Love you, Mom."

"I love you too, dear."

* * *

Before Patty could knock, Rick opened the front door. "I heard your car door shut."

Patty smiled and stepped inside. She set her overnight bag down on the floor. "Good morning, Rick."

Rick took a step forward, embraced Patty, and kissed her. "I've been looking forward to this."

Patty nodded. "Me too."

Rick picked up Patty's bag and set it on a chair in the living room. "I thought we could start our conversation here with coffee. Okay with you?"

"Very okay. Can I help?"

"No. I just want you to sit down and be served this morning. I've got muffins. Like one?"

"No, thanks. I ate breakfast, though I might want one later this morning."

Rick walked into the kitchen, poured a couple cups of coffee, added cream to hers, and joined her in the living room. They both sipped coffee in the silence.

Rick set his cup down on the end table. Their eyes locked. "Patty, there was a time in my life when I thought I'd never fall in love again. And then I met you." Rick choked up as he continued. "You helped me to heal, and since then have brought me more happiness than I deserve."

Tears formed in Patty's eyes as she listened to the words she'd longed to hear. "Rick."

Rick put up his hand. "Not yet, Patty. There's a little more I want to say. I have always believed you could do better than me, but I'm grateful you didn't find anyone else. I've hesitated moving our relationship forward because I didn't want it to interfere with our work or your career. But, aside from everything else, I don't want to go another day without knowing that you'll be with me for the rest of my life." He stuck his hand between the couch cushions, pulled out a small box, and opened it to reveal an engagement ring.

"Oh, Rick! That's beautiful!"

He stood up and extended his hand toward Patty. She took his hand and let him pull her up off the couch. Rick took hold of her left hand and slipped the ring on her finger. "Patty, will you marry me?"

Patty reached out and embraced Rick. She looked into his loving eyes. "Yes, I'll marry you, Rick. I've loved you since the first day we worked together. And I've been in love with you for the past several years. I've been afraid of caring too much for fear someone would come between us. You've just made me very, very happy."

After a long embrace and kiss, Patty stepped back. She pulled a pen and a small notepad from her purse. "Should we continue with our planning conversation?"

Rick smiled. "I hope you keep us both organized. Let's go sit at the kitchen table. Then, after our discussion, I'd like to celebrate. Just the two of us."

"I'd like that, Rick."

Rick sat down. "Let's start the list with you moving in with me."

"Me moving in with you? I assumed that you would move in with me."

Silence filled the air.

"Oh," said Rick. "I guess it's a good thing we're talking about our plans."

Patty's creased forehead gave her a worried look. "It is. I guess I was thinking that we could live in my house. I've had it for twenty years, and Becky grew up there."

Rick listened attentively. "That is the house you, your ex, and Becky lived in together."

Patty gave a nod. "It was, though only for a couple of years before he left. Does that bother you?"

"Honestly, no. It doesn't bother me. I thought it might bother you. Can you leave thoughts of him out of our marriage if we're living in the same house?"

"I'm beginning to understand your concern, Rick. I think I can, but it's not something I've previously considered. We could hold on to both places and live in my house for a while to test whether it will become a problem."

Rick drank more of his coffee. He then took Patty's hand in his. "Then I'll move in with you, and we'll see how things go."

Patty smiled. "Thank you, Rick. I will definitely let you know if our living there together creates a problem for me. I just have one question."

"Shoot."

Patty grinned. "How soon can you move in?"

"As soon as possible after Chuck settles into his condo. Will that work for you?"

"That's perfect. Tomorrow, I'll let Bec and Mom know our plans. Today is all ours."

Rick squeezed Patty's hand. "Now that we've made our plans, I vote for getting on with our day."

Patty smiled and set down her coffee cup.

CHAPTER 28

Monday morning Patty and Rick went into the interview room where Crystal was seated. Her attorney sat beside her.

"Hello, Crystal. Do you know why we're here?"

Crystal exhaled loudly. "I suppose you want to ask me the same questions you asked last time, hoping I'll say something different. Well, I won't. So you're wasting your time and mine."

"A waste of time? Possibly. Let's find out." Patty sat back in her chair and Rick leaned forward. "We've got Blake, Crystal. Do you want to know where we found him?"

Crystal smugly responded, "At his girlfriend's."

Rick glanced at Patty. She smiled while staring at Crystal. "No, Crystal, not at Kelly's. We picked Blake up at his secret hiding place in Cave Junction. Want to guess what we found?"

The look on Crystal's face changed from certainty to shock as she silently processed what she'd been told. Patty placed several photos on the table and touched one of the photos with her index finger. "You must recognize this, Crystal. Blake's drug-dealing location." Patty pointed to another photo. "And this is where he keeps his lye."

Crystal looked at her attorney without responding to Patty.

Patty directed Crystal's eyes downward onto another photo. "These are the tables where Blake dismembered your husband. When you asked Blake to do that, did you insist he kill Grant before the saw blade touched his skin?"

Crystal crinkled her nose and sat back in her chair away from the photos.

"Still think you're going to walk away, Crystal?"

Before responding, Crystal glanced up and to the right. "I don't know anything about that. I've never been there. None of this has anything to do with me."

Patty left the photos laid out on the table. "Oh, we think you do, Crystal. Your name has come up several times in our conversations with Kevin and Blake. Blake's already tried bargaining with us. He'll give up the information we want in exchange for keeping him off Death Row. He's in a cell now, Crystal. And we're talking again with him next."

Crystal's attorney was clearly looking at photos of a place she knew nothing about. "You don't have to say anything. We need to talk."

A tear fell from Crystal's eye. "You're wrong. I do have to talk. I can't lose my business. It means everything to me." She looked at Patty and Rick. "What can you do for me if I give you information on Blake and Kevin? Can you keep me out of prison?"

Patty collected the photos. "I don't know what we can do for you. It depends upon the information you have and whether the DA wants to cut a deal. Tell us what you know."

Crystal and her attorney were silent. Patty and Rick waited for a response.

A few minutes passed before the attorney broke the silence. "Come on, Crystal. We need to talk before you say anything more to them."

Crystal quietly disagreed. "No, they're talking with Blake next. If anyone is going to get a deal, it's going to be me."

The attorney leaned toward Crystal. "I can't help you if you're not going to listen."

Crystal looked at Patty and Rick. "I need to know. Can you keep me out of prison if I tell you who killed Grant and Bella?"

"We can't promise anything. The most we can do is ask the DA to be lenient. I can assure you that if the DA does show some leniency to one of you, it will be to whomever talks first."

Crystal sat back in her chair with her hands in her lap, staring at them while seemingly deep in thought. She looked up at Patty. "Okay. It was Kevin and Blake. Kevin met Blake at his place and killed Grant. Then the two of them discussed how to get rid of Bella."

"How did Blake get Grant there?"

"Blake called Grant and asked him to build a house for him. He invited Grant up to see the building that had to be demolished and talk about the new place."

Patty sat back in her chair. "Are you saying you had nothing to do with Grant's death?"

"That's right. Oh, I'm sure I told Blake more than once that Grant made me mad enough to kill him, but I didn't mean it literally." Crystal laughed. "I mean, of course, I didn't want him to actually kill Grant."

Patty observed the calmness Crystal exhibited, all the while lying about the death of her husband.

"And Bella?"

Crystal once again spoke matter-of-factly. "Kevin killed Bella. Plain and simple. He put deadly mushrooms in her soup." She stopped talking, and there was silence in the room.

A couple of minutes passed before she continued. "That's it. Now you know as much as I know." She looked at her attorney. "I'd like to go now."

Rick shook his head. "You're a bad liar, Crystal."

He and Patty were preparing to leave when Crystal's attorney advised the detectives, "You have no evidence to tie my client to the murders, therefore, in the future, call me if you have any more questions."

* * *

There was pie in the break room when the detectives and Chuck returned to the office.

Patty filled their coffee cups. "Let's talk again with Kevin about the location of the body. Given what we now know, we probably have more leverage with him than we do with Blake."

Rick stuck his fork in his pie. "I agree, but let's eat our pie first."

Patty smiled. "Agreed."

The detectives took the drive up north to the jail. Kevin sat with his hands cuffed and ankles shackled. He looked thinner as he stared at the tabletop. His attorney sat next to him.

"Hello, Kevin. We've been talking with Crystal. She says the murders are all the fault of you and Blake. Tell us about the first time you helped them. You said the woman's name was Penny Rich."

Kevin didn't look up. "Who?"

"Penny Rich. She was the woman you helped murder before Grant Wellingham."

"I didn't help murder her. I just helped Blake bury her."

"Can you describe the location where you buried her body parts?"

"Not really. It was in the dirt and sand somewhere between Harris Beach and Whaleshead. I don't remember exactly. I can't do this anymore."

"That's okay, Kevin."

Kevin looked up inquisitively. "Did Crystal tell you that she murdered the woman?"

"She's told us a lot, Kevin. There's no proof that she killed Penny Rich intentionally. That could reduce the crime and Crystal's sentence."

"You mean she might not go to prison?"

"That's a possibility."

Kevin looked up at Patty and Rick. "I have the proof you need."

Rick looked up from his notes. Patty asked, "What do you mean by proof?"

"I have an email from Crystal. It was before she became such a stickler about discussing our plans only in conversation."

"What does the email say?"

"It's from Crystal to me, and it says that she plans to kill Penny Rich. She wrote that Blake was going to help and that she needed me to work with Blake."

"Why didn't we find this email on your computer, Kevin?"

"Because I printed it out and then changed email addresses. When I bought a new computer for my job, I asked the computer tech to delete everything associated with the old email address. Then I destroyed the computer. I'm sure the email could be found if someone wanted to dig that deep into my past."

"Where did you put the printed email?"

"It's in my bank safety deposit box. I'll give you the combination. There is no way Crystal isn't going to suffer for what she's done to me."

Rick took down the combination and bank information.

"Thank you, Kevin," said Patty before leaving. "I will let the DA know what you've given us."

The detectives found the email, and it was as damning as Kevin described.

"We've got her," said Patty. "I'll let the LT know and then we can arrest her."

Rick prepared to leave. "I'll contact Brad and Pete for backup."

After returning to her office, Patty spoke to the lieutenant.

"Come in, O'Toole. Judging from your pace, I'm guessing you've got good news."

"I do, LT. We've got the evidence we need to arrest Crystal."

"Tell me what you have."

Patty shared the conversation she and Rick held with Kevin.

"That's great, O'Toole. Good work."

"Thanks."

Patty and Rick drove to the CLW Real Estate office and found Crystal in her office on the phone with a prospective client. She heard the detectives' arrival and leaned her head out the office door to see who had come in. She spoke to the person on the phone. "Let me call you back. Something urgent has come up."

Crystal stepped out into the hall. "I won't talk with you, Detectives. Not without my attorney."

Patty nodded to Rick. "We're not here to ask questions, Crystal. We're here to arrest you for the murder of Penny Rich."

Rick put handcuffs on Crystal. The energy she exhibited stepping out of the office deflated, like a balloon stuck with a pin. She was taken to jail and booked.

On the way there, Crystal called her attorney, and he agreed to meet her at the jail. Rick and Patty waited until her attorney arrived before asking questions.

Crystal now appeared pale and tired. Horizontal creases lined her forehead.

"Hello, Crystal," said Patty. "You look like you have not been sleeping well. Guilt keeping you up at night?"

Crystal squinted her eyes. "Just ask your questions so that I can go home."

"I'll get right to the point, Crystal. We've just discovered the weapon Blake used to kill your husband. Kevin has confessed to his involvement in the murders of both Grant and Bella. He, like Blake, has assured us that you were involved from the beginning."

Crystal continued to sneer at Patty. "They can say anything they want. I've already told you that I had nothing to do with those murders."

"What about the third murder, Crystal?"

Crystal jerked in her seat. "I don't know anything about a third murder."

"I think you do, Crystal. I think you were the instigator behind that one too. Kevin's told us everything. And it will be that murder that puts you away for a very long time."

"If you had anything on me, you'd have arrested me before this."

"That's not exactly true, Crystal. We've had hearsay from Blake and Kevin for days. But what we have now is solid evidence, much better than hearsay."

"What are you talking about?"

Patty put the email down in front of Crystal. "Read it, Crystal."

Crystal read it and quickly looked at her attorney before looking back at Patty. "Where did you get this?"

"Kevin gave that to us. He said that it was after that email that you began insisting that all planning had to be verbal. He's kept it all these years in the event you ever turned on him. I guess he's a little smarter than you thought."

Crystal panicked and looked at her attorney. "I want to make a deal."

The attorney paused before asking, "Will you excuse us?"

Rick and Patty left the room. Five minutes passed before an officer let the detectives know they could proceed with the questioning.

Silence filled the interview room until the attorney spoke. "She'll tell you about the murder, but she wants her sentence reduced to manslaughter with a term of no more than two years and time off for good behavior."

Patty's face showed no emotion. "We need to know what happened first. Then we'll consult the DA."

The attorney nodded to Crystal. "Go ahead."

Crystal took a couple of deep breaths before speaking. "Well, it's kind of a long story. Blake and I first met about fifteen years ago. We were kind of into drugs. Then, one night we met this woman at a party, and the three of us got stoned. She knew of a house where the family was away for the week. We left the party, broke into the house, and stole a bunch of stuff. We were never caught. Everything would have been fine if that same woman hadn't shown up here a couple of years ago. She threatened to go to the police and put information on Facebook about our involvement in the burglary and drugs."

Patty interrupted. "Threatened you?"

Crystal wiped a tear from her eye. "Yes, threatened. She was going to ruin my business. She wanted money. A lot of money. We told her that we didn't have it and asked her to just let it go. But she was broke and ready to tell all if we didn't pay her."

The detectives sat quietly and waited for Crystal to continue. She looked at the attorney who nodded in agreement.

"So Blake and I discussed the situation, and we both agreed that we needed to take some kind of action. First, we'd offer the woman a job working with Blake, provided she'd promise not to tell anyone about what we'd done. And if that didn't work, we'd have to do something to scare her. We had to protect ourselves. You know?"

Crystal waited for a response from Patty, which didn't come.

"So I invited this woman over to my house for drinks with me and Blake. I explained what Blake and I had agreed to, and Blake offered her a job."

"What kind of job?" asked Patty.

"Well, you already know that Blake does a bit of drug-selling when he's not working at the church. He'd teach her how to go about getting customers and then give her a cut of the take. Well, she laughed when he made the offer. Then she repeated her threat of going to the police if we didn't come up with fifteen thousand then and five thousand a month for an undetermined amount of time." Crystal threw her hands up in the air. "Can you imagine? How could we agree to that? Have you ever come across anyone so greedy and self-serving?"

Patty glanced at Rick before responding to Crystal. "So what did you do?"

"I offered her a drink and put a little ricin in it. My hope was to make her sick enough to realize that we were serious. She needed to go away." Crystal shrugged and exhaled loudly. "I guess I gave her a little too much. I felt terrible, but it did solve our problem."

"And that's when you called Kevin?"

"Yeah, well, not immediately. It was the next day, or maybe the day after that, when she died. I told Kevin that I just needed his help with moving the body, and that I'd cut him in on my next two commissions. He was pretty needy back then."

Rick looked up from his notes. "What did you do with the body?"

"The body? Oh yeah, that was Blake's idea. He said he knew how to take care of the problem. Then he and Kevin drove to the beach where they buried her."

"Can you show us the place where she was buried?"

"No, I wasn't with them. But Blake or Kevin could. Blake assured me that it was a location no one ever goes."

Rick glanced at Patty in time to see her roll her eyes.

Patty studied Crystal. "So you involved this woman in your drug life and then killed her when she became a threat?"

"That's pretty much it. But remember, regardless of what my email to Kevin says, my intent was not to kill her. It was to make her sick enough to leave us alone."

"What was her name?"

Crystal didn't hesitate. "Penny Rich."

"Does Penny have family here?"

"No. I think her relatives are in Nevada."

Patty looked at the attorney. "We're done here."

Crystal smiled. "I hope my information helped. When will you talk with the DA about reducing my crime?"

The detectives left the room.

CHAPTER 29

Brad intercepted them on the way back to their office.

"What's up?" asked Patty.

"It's your witness, Kevin. We just got a call that he suicided."

"How?"

"Hung himself."

Patty looked at Rick. "Hung himself in his jail cell?"

"When?" asked Rick.

"He was found this morning."

"Okay. Thanks."

The detectives were silent as they sat down at their desks and ruminated on the information Brad had just laid on them. Patty broke the silence.

"He assists with two murders, kills his wife, and then commits suicide. Are you as surprised as I am?"

Rick sat back in his chair. "After more than two decades in this people business, nothing surprises me. Suicidal thoughts may be brought on by a major life transition such as the death of a loved one, loss of a job, or the end of a relationship. Any situation that may leave people feeling overwhelmed, desperate, hurt, or helpless."

"I can see," said Patty, "how he may have decided to end his life rather than deal with the fallout of three murders. The only people in his life that he trusted used him and then turned on him."

"I'm sure," said Rick, "that the circumstances of his guilt in participating in the murders would definitely have caused him to feel hopeless desperation. Coupled with that, the prospects of him surviving unharmed in prison were nil. He was a small guy with no defensive skills. His mind probably conjured up thoughts far more painful than dying."

"I know, Rick, that Kevin was guilty of being an accomplice to horrendous crimes, and I definitely wanted him off the street. So why is this so unsettling?"

"When is the last time you had a suicide in the jail?"

Patty shook her head. "I can't remember a prior suicide in our county jail."

"Well, I understand that this first suicide in the jail can be difficult for you, but according to a 2019 study, suicides account for about thirty percent of deaths in local jails. It's been a while since I've looked up the stats on it, but I believe it may still be the leading cause of death in US jails."

Patty paused before going on. "It's interesting that he didn't hang himself until after giving us the email. He wanted to die knowing that Crystal would face prison time. I guess our county has just been fortunate up until now not to have been included in those statistics."

"Yeah. We can thank him belatedly for that. Ready to get back to work?"

Patty nodded. "The jail will handle finding Kevin's relatives. Before we get started, it's after noon and I'm hungry. I want to get my sandwich out of the refrigerator. Did you bring something to eat?"

"I didn't bring anything with me, but I'm sure I'll find some sustenance in the break room."

Patty got her sandwich while Rick picked up several cookies.

"Would you like for me to order lunch from the deli?"

Rick looked at the cookies in his hand. "No. This will tide me over until dinner."

"We've got enough to put Crystal and Blake away," said Patty, "but it feels like we're missing something." She took a bite of her sandwich while Rick sipped coffee.

"I agree. Let's go through what we've got on each of them. I'll start with

Crystal." Rick stood up and walked over to the window where the morning fog blocked his view of anything more than fifty feet away. "We've got her for the Penny Rich murder based upon her own confession and Kevin's email. The email provides proof that it was premeditated. Her guilt in the other two murders is not as easy to prove."

Patty nodded. "Based upon hearsay by Blake and Kevin, we have her as an accomplice to the deaths of both her husband and Bella but no actual evidence."

"None of the murders would have taken place without Blake," said Rick. "With discovery of the knife, we have proof that he murdered Grant. I think that the call we found on his and Kevin's cell phones the evening Bella died will, in conjunction with Kevin's statement, be enough to convict him on being an accomplice in that murder."

Patty put down her pen. "So where does that leave us? Blake denies being involved with the Penny Rich death. And Crystal denies being a participant in the deaths of both Grant and Bella. It will be difficult, based solely on testimony by the other two, to prove that she was directly involved in those murders."

Patty ate the last bite of her sandwich. She closed her eyes. "Let me think for a minute. A thought is working its way through my mind."

Rick walked back to his desk, sat down, and waited.

Patty suddenly opened her eyes and opened the file. "I know what it is!" She thumbed through the pages until she found the search warrant receipt for Blake's shed. "The castor beans."

Rick hesitated before asking. "Beans?"

"That's it, Rick. Forensics found castor beans in Blake's shed. Ricin is what's left over after processing castor beans. I'm betting the mortar and pestle will have castor bean residue on it. He provided the ricin Crystal gave to Penny Rich."

Rick smiled. "We've got him."

Patty closed the file. "This will provide us with the necessary evidence to charge and get a conviction on Crystal and Blake for all three murders. Neither of them should see the light of day for a long time. We need one more conversation with each of them."

CHAPTER 30

Blake sat quietly across from the detectives. His attorney sat beside him.

The detectives walked into the room and sat down.

Patty set a file down on the table and opened it. She pulled out an evidence envelope enclosing an open three-by-five packet of castor seeds, also identified as castor beans. She placed the envelope in front of Blake. "Do you recognize these?"

Blake remained silent.

"Of course you do. These were on a shelf in your backyard shed, along with your carrot seeds. Forensics is putting together now a list of every tool in your shed used to process these seeds into ricin."

Blake fidgeted in his chair but remained silent.

"You told us that you had nothing to do with the death of Penny Rich. That your only part in her murder was to get rid of the body. Crystal, by the way, had given you up before we came across these beans."

Blake looked coldly into Patty's eyes. "Crystal will say anything to save her own skin."

"Oh," said Patty, "I think you've misunderstood. Crystal has admitted to giving the ricin to Penny Rich. And she told us that you gave her the ricin. It's just that we had no way of tying the ricin to you until now. This now makes you guilty of first-degree murder in the death of Penny Rich."

Blake looked up at the ceiling and mumbled to himself.

Rick smiled. "This has been like a game, hasn't it? I mean, it's sort of a contest between you and Crystal. Which one of you can do the most damage to the other? You are both going away for a very, very long time. But who gets out first? Who gets to spend their last few years on this earth outside of prison?"

Blake watched Rick as he continued to speak.

"So we now have you for the murders of Grant Wellingham and Penny Rich. We believe our evidence will also make you an accomplice to Kevin in the Bella Lacky murder.

"Crystal is guilty of murdering Penny Rich and she's an accomplice in the other two deaths. So, it seems, there is no winner."

The last suggestion was more than Blake could take. He pounded his fist on the table. "She just couldn't leave well enough alone. If she hadn't brought that Kevin guy into our business, we'd have lived in peace for the rest of our lives. She just got too greedy."

CHAPTER 31

The detectives drove back to Brookings and were greeted by the lieutenant when they walked into the station. "I'd like you to follow me into the break room."

Patty glanced at Rick, then followed the lieutenant. In the break room they were congratulated by several other officers. As they looked around the room, they spotted Chuck standing off to the side. The lieutenant got everyone's attention.

"Good work, Detectives. You've removed three very dangerous killers from our streets and solved a cold case while you were at it."

Patty and Rick each shook the lieutenant's hand. "Thanks, LT," said Patty. Rick nodded. "Thanks."

Patty then addressed the group. "Rick and I couldn't have accomplished this without the hard work and assistance from all of you, and from our good friend, Chuck Spencer. Our thanks to you all for this outcome."

After talking briefly with everyone in the room, the detectives walked back to their office where Chuck joined them.

"I've got what I need from home and have purchased a table and chairs for my condo. How about the two of you come over this evening for that congratulatory dinner we discussed? Now we'll have more than one event to celebrate."

Rick looked at Patty and she smiled. "We'd love that, Chuck." Her cell phone vibrated, and Patty saw that it was her mother. "It's Mom. Give me a minute."

After the call Patty announced that Maggie wanted everyone over for Sunday dinner.

The lieutenant entered the room, walked over to a chair, and sat down.

"What can we do for you, LT?"

"From you and Rick, nothing at the moment. I'm here to make a request of Chuck."

Chuck's eyebrows rose. "Sure, LT. What is it you need?"

"Crime has picked up across the country over the past few years. And after these last murders, I'm concerned about the future. We certainly don't have the population requirement for a large SWAT team, but I would like to have a small group of our officers trained in Special Weapons and Tactics. After fifteen years working SWAT in Boston, I'm sure that you are more than qualified to take on such a team. You can name your hours and days. There doesn't need to be a commitment on your part other than what you write up for the task. Is this something you can do for us?"

Chuck stood up and walked across the room. He turned and looked at Rick, Patty, and then the lieutenant. "Let me think about it this evening, and I'll let you know tomorrow."

"Tomorrow will be good, Chuck."

Patty and Rick gathered their things to leave for the day.

"I'd like to go home and freshen up before dinner," said Patty.

"It would be good for me to do that too," Rick said. "How about I pick you up at six?"

"I'll be ready. Chuck, do you already have something in mind for dinner or can we pick up takeout?"

Chuck looked at Patty as though he'd been deep in thought. "Yeah. I have steaks."

"Okay. How about Rick and I bring the salad and bread? We can be at your place about six thirty."

Chuck smiled. "Works for me. I'm looking forward to your helping me celebrate my new home on the ocean."

Rick put his hand on Chuck's shoulder. "We are too."

I would be remiss in my acknowledgements of those who contributed to this book if I did not give thanks to my brother, Hugh Holden. It was Hugh who, during a casual conversation, provided me with information on mushrooms, both the safe and the poisonous varieties. I did not want to cause a 'spoiler alert' by placing this message of thanks in the front acknowledgement section. If his name seems familiar, Hugh was also my diving expert for *Murder at Macklyn Cove.*

G. A. Cockerham lives on the southern Oregon coast, the setting for her Oregon Coast murder mystery series. She is a retired financial advisor. Her husband, Bruce, is a thirty-year law enforcement veteran, and consultant for all police procedures within the series.